MW01254549

The Girl in the Middle

by

Cassidy Ferry

Al
Printe

Copyright ©2018 by Cassidy Ferry

rights reserved.

...d in the United State of America

Chapter 1

The dictionary defines 'tension' as when you are in a mental or emotional strain, or when you are in the state of being stretched tight. My own definition of it is when you're standing around the perimeter of the room, nervously waiting to find out where your new seat in Science class will be. It is hard to believe just a few moments before, I had been practically skipping into Mrs. Moon's classroom, a huge smile across my face. I expected today to be a normal Friday at Center Middle School, with me basking in my front row spot. I love being in the front row, even if I was not exactly enthusiastic about the bland astronomy unit we are currently studying. My front row seat was my throne, where I felt unique and dominant, like a teachers chosen pet. Unlike myself, all the popular kids seemed to head to the back of the room, to run as far away from their teacher as possible. But not me, this is where I had been since school started, and now, months later, where I hoped to stay.

"Happy Friday students. Today, I'm going to place you in a new seating arrangement," Mrs. Moon announced. We stood along the outskirts of the room, clutching our binders, laptops, and books as if they were protective armor. The lonely desks glared back at us, crying to be sat on. I leaned against the wall, and dread spilt over me like spilled water on my sketchbook. A new seating chart is any student's worst nightmare, but especially to a person like me.

Mrs. Moon walked to the back of the room, and the tension grew like a building wave ready to crush upon the innocent sand below. She faced the back row, with her teachers pointer finger out and ready to fire.

Imagine yourself in the climax of a movie, with a villain rising. I was the protagonist, in agonizing pain, Mrs. Moon controlling it. The smirk on her face made me want to crumple like a piece of paper. I stared at the last three people left. Clevis, the distracting and somewhat demented class clown, and to Coraline, the goth girl with FAILING grades. I gulped, glancing at the last three open seats. Well, I lived a decent fourteen years.

"Coraline, Clevis, and let's put Minnie in the middle!"

The science class is on Earth, while myself, Coraline, and Clevis are on another planet. Now, and forever, I'm in the back row, two monkeys sitting left and right of me. I am a lone wolf.

I'm just the girl in the middle.

A tragedy happened on December 2nd, 2016. That day, I needed a paramedic, a doctor, or perhaps an aggressive lawyer, and all because of being assigned a new seat in Science. This pointless seating chart is more unpleasant than...war or any other fill-in-the-blank catastrophe you can think of.

You can see how much of a struggle it would be for me to no longer be in my usual, treasured front-and-center seat. Long days turned into longer weeks, and every time I walked through the door to Science, I slumped into my seat and wanted to cry. Sitting in between Coraline d Clevis is like being on both sides in a World War, because they hate ther as much as I despise this. The endless fighting went on every single day for two weeks, and of course, Mrs. Moon never notices. She is one of the most laid back teachers I had ever met. With every day passing, I'm on a spaceship, sailing farther from reality. The three of us are on a completely different planet than the rest of the class. As December 13th approaches, and I am still stranded on Jupiter, where nobody else is seen.

I stood outside the Science room door, alone. I peek inside to see Mrs. Moon, who is also by herself. Every Tuesday after lunch, I would come early to class. Before the two clowns would come in, I would relish the silence, and relax a little. I strolled into the room today and took a seat, listening to the sound of peaceful bliss. The quiet makes this my favorite time of day. Mrs. Moon cracks her window open, adding the soft sounds of winter birds chirping, a gentle breeze. It sure isn't the sound of constant bickering between Clevis and Coraline. I listen to the pattern of Mrs. Moon's typing on her computer. Soon, there is a slight pause, and she peers at me.

"Hello Minnie, how are you?" Mrs. Moon asked.

"Well, I'm fine," I answered, but what I want to say is when I can reclaim my lost seat, I'll be better then fine. It seems so far away. People could only dream of getting into the back row, because they can do whatever their little hearts desire. Back here, students doodle on their worksheets, they text each other, and people don't pay attention in class. Add this to the list I wrote of reasons why I despise the back row. By the time I finish this list, the paper will extend out to the moon. Miles of long bullets on why this new arrangement is ruining my life.

I slouched back and stared at the surroundings in the room. We are doing the study of astronomy all year, and posters are everywhere, along with star models, cardboard asteroids, and comets, and the main eight planets hung from the ceiling. They're arranged so each of them got colder as they reached the back of the room. Ironically, I'm sitt' next to the coldest planet of them all. Actually, Pluto isn't considered a planet anymore, just like my inner front row person. This modeled dwarf planet is like my little seat in the middle, because it's barely noticed.

My eyes traveled to the window, away from the freezing planets. Perched on there, stood a single owl. Just a ghost like owl with unmistakable white, like an angel from the depths of heaven. This must come out of my imagination, or a hallucination, or an illusion is appearing right in front of my eyes. This snowy owl is so lifelike like it is almost real. I stared in absolute shock. I closed my eyes, and when they opened again, nothing is there.

"There is about a week until our ice skating field trip. Please remember to turn in your permission slips, sooner than later, and tomorrow, I will give you additional details. Another thing, winter vacation starts the day after, so we're going to lay back for the next few days. For today, we will be watching a video of possible life on other planets," Mrs. Moon delightfully informed. I banged my head on the desk, and hoped for this class to be over. On a brighter note, Coraline and Clevis are being quiet for once.

I turned my head to Coraline. She is on her flip phone, searching pictures of skeletons and her smile broadened when blood appeared on the skulls. She is... one of a kind, in a different way from 'one of a kind'. She doesn't belong to a kind, meaning she is different from the whole school. She's been failing her classes, and she spends her free time being the troublemaker she is. If I placed her somewhere in this lar system, it would be in the core of the sun, because she is burning lf with each day passing. With her black graphic t-shirts and half

GOOD THINGS

- ○ ....
- ○ ....
- ○ ....
- ○ ....
- ○ ....
- ○ ....
- ○ ....
- ○ ....
- ○ ....
- ○ ....
- ○ ....
- ○ ....
- ○ ....
- ○ ....
- ○ ....
- ○ ....
- ○ ....
- ○ ....
- ○ ....

Measure success by how many
happy memories you've made.

shaved head, I bet she owns a motorcycle, and rides it without a license. She is riding her way into getting caught on her phone, but if I am her, I wouldn't care. In fact, she is the one who starts fights with Clevis, like the British in the Revolutionary War. They are killing each other and fighting for independence. Clevis compared to Coraline is like night and day. Positive and negative, win or lose right and left, even life and death.

I rolled my head to the other side, where Clevis sat. Unlike Coraline, Clevis is one of a kind. He thinks of himself as the class clown, but in reality, he is a bucket load of distractions. His shaggy hair always swung over his face, then there are the glasses, braces, and the Charlie Brown type of face. He reminds me of a puppy who hops around, knocking over antiques in your house. He barks at the top of his lungs, and you can never catch a break with him, chiefly when he randomly shouts out in class. So he may have some sort of a problem. Obviously, this annoys Coraline, and indeed, hence the constant bickering.

"Min, let's pull a little prank on Clevis and make him think a ghost is in here," Coraline proposed.

"Well.. I don't want to get in trouble, but if you want to take that risk...,"

"Clevis. Have you ever heard of the myth of the ghost in the back of the science room? Legend has it a ghost flies around in the back of the room, particularly when it's dark and cold outside," Coraline tells him, like an evil southern witch, who cackles almost every minute. Clevis appeared to be scared as he searched around. Darkness spoiled the inside, and the chill touched my innocent soul.

"Minnie, is this true?"

I pause, wondering why 'no' isn't coming out of my mouth. I am hesitant on whether to cause a little mischief, OR, to continue as being the responsible one in this group. I'm known for not answerin questions, and being forgot in this class... at least in this seating arrangement. Things could change for the better or worse, if I could do something for once.

"Yes, the legend is true." Coraline smiles at me, grimly like her grim self. Come on, nobody's perfect, not even me. Clevis stares into blank space, fear, yet silence, etched on his face. That's a change... he's never silent for this long. Seconds later, he shivers, growing paler like he's in the freezing ocean, getting bit by tiny fishes, and stung by glowing jellyfish. Clevis is a ghost... and yes... hence the dramatic change.

"Ghost... GHOST! GHOST!!! GHOST INSIDE THE ROOM!!" He shrieked, with full fake phobia. All of a sudden, Clevis threw binders on the floor, while holding one up to his face. He kicked and punched the air like a young kid who found out the tooth fairy isn't real. Instantly with expectation, every person turned their head, except Mrs. Moon, who fell asleep at her desk. Change isn't good all the time, especially when it comes to Clevis, or a seating chart, or middle school, or anything for this matter. Well actually, here's a change; I'm inwardly enjoying it. These kinds of things never brought a smile to my face, but that only made this moment more momentous.

Clevis continued to scream, like a devil is about to kidnap him. I can imagine Coraline opening a sack, pushing Clevis in and taking him underground. Wait, we already are in hell.

"HELP ME!!!" he yelped. "HELP, HELP, help, help me!!!"

And he believed it. Even though I'm "the super glue," or, "the silent leader," he reacted the way he did and I couldn't help but laugh my ankles off because of it. It's humorous to see how an eighth grader is freaking out over a childish rumor.

Eventually, Mrs. Moon took notice of this incident, and moved Clevis to the place I can only dream about. The front row called our ~~es~~, although, this isn't bad. Coraline and I giggled inside ourselves, throughout the rest of the period.

The temperature is bound to hit freezing sooner or later. For the longest time, I wished for the darkness of rain to turn into the light of snow. January is nearing, and not one speck of snow has fallen to the ground. Everyday, I wanted to look out the window, and to see big, small, snazzy, short, tall, pretty, petty, fresh, frenzy, snow. For the past few weeks, walking into a gloomy room without snow outside was depressing. Well, hail turned into a snowflake after the 'ghost incident' yesterday. This isn't ideal, yet, no seating chart will be flawless. Ever since I let out my dark side, a new light entered.

"Hey Minnie!!!!! Aren't you so excited?? Today is hump day!!!!!" Clevis, slightly blushing with his innocent gaze at me. I smirked, greeting my fellow troublemaker. He started peering, and I gazed over him. We are only gaping at each other, and nothing else like this happened before, not in my life. I can't keep eye contact for this long. Just me, myself and I, staring into his hazel tinted eyes. These are the moment's everyone is talking about, like when you find true love. Yes... I will die of embarrassment if this keeps going. A world of neglect and animosity will enter my treacherous life, and it will turn out to be a dilemma, lasting a millennia. I'm not sure what words to say, except for "thank you Coraline", when she trudged through the door.

She came in slouching, dark strands of hair covering her frowning face. "I reckon we got the computers today. This outta be a boring class."

Mrs. Moon gave Coraline a glare after she 'accidentally' let out a swear. She marched to the front of the room, the class concluded chatting about the latest gossip, and Clevis stopped staring at me. The middle walkway of the room is like the red carpet of Hollywood to Mrs. Moon. While walking through it, everyone gave her attention. Althoug Mrs. Moon may look strict at times, strolling through the rug with h devilish frizzy hair, shady black eyes, and sly smiles, she is actually the one teacher who every child favors. Mrs. Moon understands drama in our generation, yet, she did put me in that seating chart, which I don't appreciate.

"Two quick things before we start. First, don't forget to hand in the form for ice skating next week. This is important to turn in because it's our only non-educational field trip for the whole year. We'll be taking two buses there, skating for three hours, and watching movies for the rest of the day. Sixty forms are already in my hand, so for those thirty people, BRING IT IN. For today, take out your computers and open the link I posted on the board. It's a game where you can find different kinds of galaxies, virtually," she directed. "You will be able to see when that certain galaxy was formed, and how many light years away it is. If you need help, I will be coming around the room," she explained.

While awaiting for my computer to load, I ripped out a scrap of paper, and doodled. Most of the time, I don't do that because I pay attention in class... however, it's okay once in awhile, like when you're waiting for your old school laptop to work. First I tell a lie to Clevis, and now this! I am becoming a troublemaker. As I moved my pencil along the fragment of paper, a tiny owl started to form, like the snowy owl I spotted yesterday. People say I'm great with that kind of stuff. They say I have a creative mind, a gift to cherish, a present to show the world.

"MINNIE!!!! THAT IS EXTRAORDINARY!!!!" Clevis admired, blushing even more. I realized I am reddening myself. Clevis gave me a charming smile, while my face turned into a cherry tomato.

"Thank you."

My computer finished loading and I found the game. As more formation processed into my brain, I figured out the meaning of this . It's educational, and it is still a game and so, Clevis worshiped it... a little too much though. Whenever he obtained a new galaxy, he would scream with delight. "I DISCOVERED THE MILKY WAY GALAXY!!!!!"

I thought he's overreacting this one minute. I should've known... I am far from being right.

Clevis continued to screech throughout the entire period, and other people started complaining after a while. One person said they felt bad for me and Coraline, while other people went to Mrs. Moon. She didn't do anything, being the laid back teacher she is. His yelling and over exaggerating got more constant as he escalated to higher levels, and to a point where I needed a massage.

"I FOUND A.... RARE ONE.... OH MY GOODNESS... MY GOD.....LOOK AT WHAT I SPOTTED!! THIS IS SO AWESOME!!!!"

"Minnie!!! Look! I discovered an amor galaxy," he muttered, in his whisper voice. His muttering voice is more identical to a quiet shout, like when you want someone to hear something, or when you're trying to draw attention to yourself.

"Mrs. Moon should do something about this, it is getting annoying," Coraline jeered. We both looked at Mrs. Moon with plead in our eyes, and she came over. She kneeled down between our desks. "Clevis, you can be quiet now. I think we've all had enough."

"Sorry Mrs. Moon, I'll stop now. Besides, I'm almost done."

"Thank you," I sighed, not realizing how red my face is, and how I'm twirling my hair. He gave an apologetic smile. My ears needed a break, but my heart is still beating like the fast ticking of a clock.

Coraline pulled her head off the desk and grinned, knowing the hurricane is over. Clevis stopped screaming, and he started doodling. Now I'm waiting for the blizzard season to commence. I stared the window. Clouds are whiter and the sky is nowhere to be seen. Brightness filled the whole room, like heaven is flying through the window

The darkness Coraline brought is gone, and a new light entered. There, I discerned something, something microscopic only as far the eye can see. Something with pattern and crystallized holes on the sides, something making me gleam and beam with joy and jubilation. This reminds me of the time I cut out paper snowflakes for Christmas last year. Then, I realized exactly what I am staring at.

The first snowflake of winter. It trickled to the ground, and gently landed on a strand of grass. With one snowflake on the loose, more are coming. Waiting for this moment was depressing, but here it is.

A few minutes later, more snowflakes came trickling down the horizon. It is getting brighter and soon, snow came floating downwards. Snowflakes of all diverse shapes and sizes, like big, small, snazzy, short, tall, pretty, petty, fresh, frenzy, snow. Snowflakes are like people in the world. Clevis is a special snowflake. A loud snowflake, an obnoxious snowflake, or even, a snowflake with many different textures... I liked it.

I raced over to the window next to Mrs. Moon's desk. She's gazing over the outdoors, and her face's glowing from the reflection of winter's call. "We're like kids on Christmas morning, especially when it comes to the first snowfall of the season," I said to her. "We are, we really are," She whispered back. This is extraordinary. She smiled at me, reminding me of the owl, and Clevis, who may not be the person who I thought he is.

As the clock struck 1:00, the bell rang. Instead of complaining to Mrs. Moon about this pointless arrangement, I studied the flakes of snow, like I dreamed of from time to time. To steal from Charles Dickens, it is the best of times, but it is also the worst of times. To Clevis, it is the age of foolishness, but it could turn out to be the age of wisdom. For Coraline, it is the epoch of belief, but it is the epoch of incredulity. s of myself, it is the season of Light, it is the season of Darkness. And 'ese famous words apply to the new seating arrangement? Yes, '+ does.

Chapter 2

The great and glorious drama club. You might expect a gigantic theater with ruby red curtains, or a golden stage floor where an actor or actress can shine like a Hollywood star. The lights made the stage look like Rockefeller Center during the Christmas season. Rows of cushioned seats with numbers on each of them. An experienced director who makes Broadway plays and musicals. Props taking days, or weeks, to paint by hand. The Lion Kings masks, Hamilton's history concepts, and the Wicked witches, who make the musical, well, wicked. Even Dear Evan Hansen and those beautiful harmonies. Aladdin, who turns that stage into a whole new world. What you may expect in a theater club.... well, that isn't us.

After school on Friday, I walked into the Center Middle School's drama club, also known as the cafeteria. The lunch tables transform into benches, and a stage built into the side. A lower quality environment is set here, but we can somehow make this into a quarter of what Broadway is. We buy our props from The Dollar Tree, and audition satisfactory actors and actresses.

We are in the beginning stages for our musical this year. Mrs. Short, the drama administrator announced last week we're doing Disney's, *Frozen*.

"When their kingdom becomes trapped in perpetual winter, fea

Anna joins forces with mountaineer Kristoff and his reindeer sidekick. Their goal is to find Anna's sister, Snow Queen Elsa, and break her icy spell. Their epic journey leads them to encounters with mythical trolls, a comedic snowman, harsh conditions, and magic at every turn. They bravely push onward in a race to save the kingdom from winter's cold grip," Mrs. Short read off the script.

"*Frozen,* the highest-grossing animated film of all time, is what we are doing this year. Everybody's seen *Frozen*, and most people like it, except for the people who despise it. We are playing this musical because even I, an adult, love this movie. As my last year of being director, after 25 years in this career, I know in my frozen heart we'll all remember it."

With Mrs. Short's reddish hair, crystal eyes, short height, and old fashioned dresses, she looks like a classic elf, just experienced enough to put on a fine performance.

I spotted Coraline and Clevis bickering with each other on stage, and I questioned why I even joined this club. Marching to the stage, I sighed, ready to meddle with some rough things.

"Hi group!" I interjected. "What's crackalackin'?" Just me and my quirky catchphrases to break the ice. Clevis stared at me, so I crossed my arms and flipped my hair. Highly unlikely for myself to pass as a popular person. Who Clevis would have a crush on.

I shattered that ice, but not in the way I expected. "Coraline, I can't believe there isn't a ghost in the back of the science room! That was MEAN," Clevis continued to yell, before I interrupted him. He turned and stomped away. Coraline's face is a ghost white, like the ghost she made up. "Hey Casper the Friendly Ghost, quick word?" I said to her.

I had the past two days to consider a relationship for Clevis and I can't stop fantasizing about him, in a different way. In Science on ʳsday and Friday, he kept staring at me, and smiling whenever I looked at him. Girl's crave these things, and I'm always thinking highly of him, like he's a king, or a male Kardashian.

I gestured Coraline to the other side of the stage, far away from where Clevis is pretending to whimper. A plan in mind is forming, the kinds of plans which make me slip into an abyss. A type of abyss you can't swim out of once you make the decision to fall through the darkness. An abyss with no end, and no visible light to be seen.

"Will you do me the biggest favor and ask Clevis who he likes?" I asked, with desperation.

"Sure, fine, but only because I want to see who he is crushing on."

This is the one time I wish she wouldn't figure out anything. In class, she struggles to calculate things. The simple science equations are a burden to her. With this concept, I'm hoping, for once, she doesn't get this right. I waved at Clevis, then gandered at Coraline and nodded my head. If this goes wrong in any way, than commence to the catalyst of DRAMA.

"So Clevis, do you have a crush on anyone?"

As Clevis pondered, my heart bounced up and down and my ankles twisted and twirled like a clown doing ballet. This made me want to grab Clevis, pull him on a stallion, and ride into the western sunset. Clevis and I, we would live on a farm. We'll grow old together, and one night, we'll be on the porch, watching the horses. Through my wrinkled eye, I'll see Clevis, right by my side, rocking his chair and jumping up and down.

"Nope," he murmured. Coraline shrugged and stared at me with more suspicion. No, I will never give up. Besides, love never accepts a defeat, no challenge it can't meet, no place it cannot go. I leaned in closer to Clevis, whispering in his ear.

"Clevis, we are asking because there is someone in this school who does like you," I muttered. I'm walking on eggshells here, and they're cracking like my future with the one and only. I turned to see Coraline shaking her head in my shame. When one of my plans goes in a different direction, it causes a game changer, or a plot twist. They can be good or bad, better or shoddy. You can think they're good, but they aren't, or you can think they're bad, but it's a great thing.

"Clevis, Minnie is totally crushing on you," Coraline divulged, figuring it out. This is a bad, bad, bad thing. I let myself drop to the stage floor, like in one of those dramatic movies when the main character falls after losing their soulmate. They'd yell "NO!!!" Even though this is drama club, I can't roar with agony. I fell, landing on a pillow filled with bricks.

Coraline shielded her mouth in the time when seeing my expression. "Impossible," she choked. Clevis' jaw flared open while letting it hang in a frozen position. The last thing I detected.... the final thing.... was the gleam in his grin, before he ran to one side. Coraline sauntered back gradually, gesturing me to come along. Coraline and Clevis are on separate sides of the stage, both wanting me to come. Once more, I am in the middle.

I looked left at Coraline. Her feet are planted into the ground. She stood up tall, like a soldier going into the army. I dug my fingernails into my skin thinking about it. Clevis kneeled with his head buried in his hands, tiny cracks to peek through. Oh, so innocent Clevis, so soft, so precious, like a newborn baby. These feelings are newborn, and love never accepts a defeat, no challenge it can't meet, no place it cannot go. I reached out my hand to the guy on the end. I didn't turn back to look at Coraline, and she's probably snarling.

"Clevis," I quivered, still reaching for him. "AH!!!"

I almost fell when taking a step back. Coraline came marching over and she slapped herself on the forehead again, in her own shame for me. "Minnie, what did you--"

"Oh Clevis, always bringing attention to himself," Victoria sassed. I should've seen her running up the stage stairs with her overly dressed wardrobe. I could mistake her for the Queen of England, with her millions of dollars in makeup and jewelry. She is the most popular person in our school, and the leader of "The Wolves," the name of the main popular group. Victoria let out a huge howl.

"This has nothing to do with you Victoria," I hissed. She ignored me and placed her pink feathery arm around Clevis. Victoria almost breathed on him, and he coughed from her perfume. "Clevis, will you tell me why you're pretending to be scared? You are embarrassing us," she said, affectionately. She squeezed his cheeks.

"Minnie likes me," he whimpered. Victoria melodramatically collapsed on the floor laughing. "No way... you can't be serious Min, Clevis is like, such a geek... if you dated him... then you will be the most unpopular girl in the school!!"

She banged her hand against the wooden stage. Tears welled up in my eyes as my face showed blotch. Clevis covered his mournful expressions. Coraline sat down, gazing over the show and eating popcorn. This is the abyss I'm talking about, an abyss full of darkness, of pity and pain, and the abyss where I, myself, where I belong in this moment. Where the drama I created is backfiring, with Victoria crying with laughter, Coraline pretending to enjoy this, and Clevis, who will never know the truth.

"Clevis.... I don't like you."

I lied to him, hiding in bitterness and regret. "Good job Minnie. You saved yourself loads of embarrassment," Victoria said. She looked relieved as she adjusted her diamond bracelet. Coraline nodded her head in agreement.

"I'm so sorry Clevis," I sniffled. Under his crooked glasses, Clevis' eyes are watery.

"I was hoping someone liked me for once, but now, nobody ever will." Clevis ran away again, and this time is different, because I let him go. A tear soaked into my shirt, and the marking laid there, like it always will.

To tell the truth, I want to live in a previous time. The golden age when children had a one hour limit on their television, while listening to CDs on their boomboxes. Back when plaid shirts and bell-bottom jeans were trends, and back when people acted like themselves. In the past, people didn't care about their followers on social media, because that wasn't invented. Maybe drama existed, but trust me when I tell you this, it was nothing like it is now. A whole new world arrived. Now, the transition from elementary to middle school is the best, yet, the worst of times.

Middle school is supposed to be the beautiful and glorious time when children are blossoming into young adults. We turn into different people as we find new passions, opportunities, and, in time, we gain character. You can decide if you want to join clubs, be a better student, and even make a difference in the world. An exciting time in life when you find those soul mates--those friends who may turn out to be the most important relationships for life. However, in the present, there is one huge obstacle: popularity. In Center Middle School, there are two main groups: the popular kids (also known as the "Wolves"), and the rest of us, who are desperate to be like them. We 'envy' Victoria in view of the fact she is leader of The Wolves. I am probably fooling myself if I think they know anything about me more than my name, which is Minnie Ann Stickley-Adotte.

"Hey Clevis, listen... I'm sorry about what happened today. You must be super mad with me, and I can comprehend if you are. The truth is, I DO like you. You are such a unique and extraordinary person. Anyway, I will understand if you don't want to be my friend. Life is tough sometimes."

I stared at my phone. After reading this message ten million times, I sent it. I hope he reads this before Monday at 9:30am, when Science takes place. I sat at my drawing desk. A gigantic piece of paper laid out, with several charcoal pencils.

As soon as my phone buzzed, I threw it on the floor. I slowly got to my knees and crawled towards it. My heart beated, and I'm like a prisoner trying to escape. To escape from an abyss I jumped into. Escape from the dark feelings and weights pulling me down. To escape what I put myself through. I picked it up, in fear by what could happen.

"Minnie, I'm not mad. I only thought for once in my life, someone liked me, but I guess I'm wrong. The only emotion I feel now is sadness," he replied.

"Same here Clevis. And, I am also sorry about Victoria. The story of popularity began all the way back to kindergarten. There would always be 'that one kid' who acted nice, but is a backstabber. Vicky snatched my bag of goldfish, and hence, a long seven years. I somehow lasted with her bullying me through elementary school and most of middle, yet, she still knows how to win every battle. Clevis, just note, never trust her. But, I'm going to admit something. I want to be popular, and to be in The Wolves. Victoria may not always be honest, but she is right. It is wrong for me to like you, so I'll ask Mrs. Moon to change our seats, and all this drama will be over," I retorted. I sent the text without re-reading.

Clevis read the message, and now my hands are shaking. "Why do you listen to Victoria?" He asked. I glanced at the clock, 10:30. I hope he clicks in his seat belt because this is going to be one of those long nights. Usually, after the third hour, I would get sick of talking to my friends. Nothing changed as I hit the fifth of talking to Clevis. For every lengthy hour, for every measured minute, and slow second, the light of day arose, little by little. I crawled up the creaking ladder, out of the abyss. Every time I considered asking him to be my boyfriend, Victoria pops up in my mind, and does what she did earlier today. My plan backfired because of the pressure of pretty and petty Victoria, always getting in the way of my happiness. Well, for every long hour, for every minuscule minute, and steady second I spent texting him, Clevis made me see the light at the end of the tunnel, and this is what I deserve.

"Clevis, before you go to bed on this Friday night, I want an answer to a question. The reply to this question will be a change for us. All our friends, enemies, classmates. This question will be like, a new seating chart, a new chapter in our life stories."

"Yes Minnie?"

"Can we be an official couple?"

"Okay."

Chapter 3

December 16th, 2016... the day a beautiful relationship was born. Reporters are approaching my house, asking questions about Clevis. "This is... shocking... astonishing, astounding... sensational... unbeliev- able.." they'll say. I'll answer hundreds of questions and comments coming with my fan mail. Then, I'll do a LIVE broadcast on NBC, and I would be the new face of television. The Senate will become en- grossed, the Judicial Branch, and for the heck of it, The President will hear about this. The United Nations will request a meeting with me, presenting many nominations and awards. I'll have my own holiday, where everyone will take the day off, and cherish Clevis and I, the new king and queen of England. Minnie Ann Stickley-Adotte... the world will adore this name. Well, I wish.

Even though Clevis and I aren't quite celebrities yet, the whole school found out quickly. People are acting like this is the royal wedding of 2011, when Prince William and Catherine Middleton got married. Their ceremony was broadcasted live on TV, but since I was in 2nd grade then, I only goggled at their kiss at the end. But now, the only thing people are goggling over is the new king and queen of Center Middle School.

From the time period of Friday at midnight, to Monday morning, my phone exploded with text messages, emails, and voicemails. In fact,

The Wolves are praising me like I am the first female president. In the mail, I got a card from Victoria, which is quite strange though, considering how she acted on Friday. By her sending that, it is more strange than the concept of Netflix's *Stranger Things*. Victoria is like a demogorgon, scary in many ways. Ignoring that, the card is as sweet as this new life. On Monday, I arrived to science early. Before class, I avoided the paparazzi in the halls. It's hard to sneak around, hiding like an agent in Mission Impossible. Out of all the surprises I received in the past few days, the biggest shock I got is how science is set up. There are no rows, groups, clusters of desks, or the stadium method. In fact, they made a gigantic square around the perimeter of the room. That only signifies one thing... no seating chart.

I scrambled to claim my long lost spot like an obsessed maniac, letting out a squeal before plotting myself in this seat. I smiled, and my eyes wandered to the window, where a single snowy owl is perched. I shook my head, with a surprise far greater than any seating chart. When her bill turned into a sly smile, I spotted an orange feather run along her tail. I never admired such a thing before this moment, making me gleam back, with my jaw hanging open. Somehow, this snowy owl is different than the rest.

I blinked once again and the owl is gone. Behind me, the door creaked open. I turned around, knowing who is standing there. Clevis is glowing like an animated jellyfish, lighting up the depths of the ocean. He is the first colored photograph, staring in the first motion picture. A blue snowflake landing in a field of pearly white, or a rose in a sunflower garden, or the pillow in the pile of blankets.

When Clevis walked down Mrs. Moon's red carpet, he was like a model in my opinion. His messy hair swayed to one side, and glasses slid down his nose. He gave me a charming smile, showing off his braces on his buck teeth. If this is a romance novel, the reader would be on the edge of their seat. The next thing people could expect is for him to lean in, and softly kiss me, because this is love.

"Hi Minnie!!!" he hollered, staggering to the front row, and dropping his books and binders on my desk. Well, that ruined the moment.

"Hello Clevis."

I relaxed, not realizing people are already walking in the room. The pleasant thing is how Clevis and I are together in the front row. My old and new dream coming true. I glanced over to my new dream who is blushing insanely, and to my nightmare, Aneska, with most enthusiastic expression implanted on her face.

"How many kids do you have?" She wondered. Aneska rocked her legs back and forth, like a kindergartner acting in Legally Blonde. Aneska and Victoria are like twins who aren't treated equally. They are best friends, but Aneska is more of a sidekick kind of friend. Aneska is Victoria's shadow, because she's always following her footsteps. She's similar to the secretary of The Wolves Pack, but she wouldn't be paid minimum wage if that is a job. Nevertheless, Aneska is popular, so the rule of thumb is too listen to her, and answer her inappropriate questions about Clevis and I having children.

"Seven kids. Our oldest is Spoon, and the youngest is Fork. The others are Knife, Tablespoon, Pot, Pan, and Spatula. We named all of them after our favorite utensils, isn't that right Clevis?" I gave him a quick wink, hoping he would agree with me, to make myself look better in front of a Wolf. He nodded his head. Clearly, Clevis doesn't care for popularity, so he also rolled his eyes.

"Good afternoon everyone!" Mrs. Moon yelled, interrupting my conversation with Aneska. "Today is a laid back day. You can do whatever your little heart's desire for the next hour. I'll be coming around, answering any questions about the ice skating field trip," she instructed. Mrs. Moon wrote some additional information on the board, and Clevis and I, we scrutinized Aneska, who claimed the desk next to me.

"Clevis, do you know how to ice skate?" she asked him. I turned to him with anticipation in my eyes. I can imagine it now. On the ice rink, my heart will be beating. As I professionally twirl on the crystal clear ice, I'll leap into the air, finding myself levitated above the ground. Clevis would wrap his hands around my waist and lift me to the skies. I'll be in the center of my own world, staring down at the person who matters most to me. Clevis will bring me down, and everyone could be applauding, like the end of Titanic when Rose is reunited with Jack in her dreams.

"Nope."

Well, that flash forward won't be a reality.

"Can you rollerblade?"

"No."

"How about roller skating? It's easier than rollerblading," I asked.

"No... never been on those... shoes with wheels and blades. "Minnie, will you teach me?"

"Sure Clevis, but I'm warning you, we will be holding hands," I said without thinking.

"That will be so adorable!!!" Aneska squealed.

Clevis smiled like how the Grinch smiles when forming his plans on stealing Christmas. "I would LOVE that." And of course, he over exaggerated the love part.

As expected, the whole class stared at him. Now and as always, this is my boyfriend, who's never been on shoes with wheels. Wednesday will be a pretty daunting feat.

"Hey little Miss Juliet!" she said "Aneska, shut up!" I gushed. Aneska and I are sitting with our lunch boxes ready, and coats on. Even though Aneska could be like a wolf sometimes, she can be kind, like a half-wolf turning into a puppy.

"Min, you'll do FINE. You look nervous, but hakuna matata, it means no worries!"

"Clevis is expecting me to teach him, but I'm not good myself,' I said to her.

The wall around the rink was my lifeguard when I was younger. When I was three years old, I had the meanest instructor, and the worst ice skating class possible. I never ended up learning anything from them, and the only thing I looked forward too was getting a donut from Dunkin Donuts after those sessions. Every time those memories popped in my mind, my fists clench, chills go down my spine, sweat breaks out, and my stomach had a migration of fluttering butterflies traveling to the south for winter, and away from the ice.

"Do you want to sit with me on the way over? We're taking two separate buses, and it is very unfortunate to hear, but I don't think Clevis will be with us," Aneska continued. It's one thing that she's talking to me, but by her asking me to be with her on the bus, that is quite strange. "Well if that is the bus arrangement...," I drawled to her, with a cheesy grin. Two buses are parked, labeled bus one and bus two. As my group traveled to bus two, I sighted bus one, which is full with all my friends, and Clevis in the window. Through the frosty glass, he put his hand up, leaving a mark in the thin ice. I waved at him, but made a depressing expression when boarding bus number two.

"No big deal! It takes five minutes to ride there anyway," Aneska commented. We hopped on the bus, and was forced to sit in the front row, next to the teachers and the bus driver with no teeth. With all these new seating arrangements lately, my feelings changed for every single one of them. No back row, yes front row, yes middle seat, no middle seat, no front row, no back row, no front bus seat, yes front bus seat. I chuckled to myself, chills going down my spine.

When I got off the bus, seeing Clevis made me more confident than ever. We hid away from The Wolves, and I helped him put on his skates. He examined me with worry etched on his face, and I smiled, telling him there was no worries, but in reality, I was as worried as a little kid getting a shot from the doctor. Clevis wobbled as we were about to enter the cold sensation. I placed my arm around him, because we need to be there for each other. He nodded at me and said "Let's do this."

"Listen Clevis, honey, you have to let go of the wall or else, sweetie, you will never make progress, sweetheart," I told him. I'm acting calm and collected, but my teeth are gritting, and making a silent squeaky chalkboard sound. I wanted to rip my blade off my skate, walk to Clevis, and convince him to let go. His body is more glued to the wall than a root is to a tree, and he is sticking on there like one of those annoying caterpillars.

"I'm sorry Minnie... I can't do this."

Clevis staggered to the entrance, and left me standing there. My skates wouldn't let me move because they were disappointed in me, as I am also downhearted in myself. I mean, things were going fine before we got to this stage.

Well, I just proved there is no such thing as beginners luck.

"Minnie! MINNIE! Minnie Ann, come over here now!!!"

I swayed over to Victoria, and her shadow, Aneska. Victoria had a wolf fur coat, white figure skating skates, the ones with those fancy laces, and fluffy earmuffs. Aneska wore the exact same thing, but in lower quality and price. They both waved me over. I'm as honored as a mother on Mother's Day. Breakfast in bed, flowers, cards, and a box of chocolates that are sweet, like The Wolves wanting to talk to me.

"How's your NEW and ADORABLE boyfriend? Do you LOVE him yet?" Victoria queried. From what I hear, "love" is a very powerful word. It is more strong than any force in the world, at least any emotional drama movie would show that. As The Wolves waited for me to answer, more Wolves gathered around, silently howling at me. Aneska and Victoria leaned in closer, breathing hard. They are either being nosy, or being somewhat subtle to me. The Wolves are being nice and I'm not feeling invisible anymore. Is this possible? Possible to conquer this impossible? Impossible to beat the possible? Possibly. This is impossible. With this going on, possibilities can pursue the impossible.

"I'm not sure about love yet."

The Wolves looked disappointed, but as for Victoria herself, she only smirked like a girl creating mischief.

"Darling, you love him," she expressed, raising her eyebrows, waiting for me to agree. I held to the wall for dear life, just like I did when I was younger. The Wolves are like the mean instructors, urging me to let go. I nodded my head, releasing myself from the side.

"See?! Minnie DOES love him," Victoria posed. Her along with the rest of The Wolves squealed, and started showering me with laughs and attention. I feel like a Wolf!

"Couple of the year! Wait, let me restate that, COUPLE OF THE CENTURY!!!" she cheered. The Wolves burst out laughing, like mimes who only guffawed in a frantic way. I smiled and rolled my eyes. It doesn't matter though, because the one and only, Victoria, gave me a compliment. It is merely possible to beat the impossible, as most cliched quotes are. Unlike those, it is kind of fun to do the impossible, as Walt Disney once stated.

"Wolves! Separate! Find Clevis! Questionnaire time!" Aneska hollered. Victoria pushed in front of her and lead The Wolves away. As soon as they were out of sight, I realized I was standing straight on these two blades. With my dad being a hockey player, and when I was younger, he told me to "push right, then stride left, and keep on doing that." So, I did, and I skated as rapid as all the Olympians in the Olympics combined, or as fast as the fastest rocket ship. I am flying like a hummingbird, waving like a flag in the wind. Adrenaline caught up to me. People are blurs. Blades struck 12:00. Agility took over. Ice swayed me. Left and right. Breathe in and out.

"YOU GO GIRL!!!" Mrs. Moon exclaimed, scaring me and making me almost fall over. My teeth are inches away from being lost, like our bus drivers. Mrs. Moon grabbed my arms right before I tumbled on the ground, and she saved me. I'm shaking, afraid this would happen. "I'm sorry! Are you okay? You are speedy out there!" Mrs. Moon apologized.

"I'm... I'm... dumbstruck, but awestruck, but struck, let me make an metaphor about this... I'm as terrified as when you PUT ME IN THAT SEATING CHART IN THE BACK ROW." She slowed down a bit and placed her hands in her sweatshirt pocket.

"Aren't you and Clevis together?"

My jaw dropped, and I let it show. "I knew it on Friday when you two in the front row, and when you two lovebirds were playing for the whole study period!"

"Yes! We are a happy and loving couple, and it's all because you put us together in science!" Clevis shouted when Mrs. Moon and I arrived at the bleachers. He is thinking the exact thing I am.

"Oh, right, that futile seating arrangement," I mocked. Mrs. Moon broke out laughing, placing her hand on my shoulder. Then she skated away, giving me a passing glance.

"Well Clevis, are you ready to try again?"

He nodded, and goggled at my hand. I wore a black glove, and eached it out to Clevis. At the moment he took it, a tingly sensation touched. Warmness from my heart throughout my entire body, shutting out the ice from outside. I gripped a little tighter and went along with Clevis leaning on me for support. He wouldn't let go, but this is a start. "Soon, you'll be flying at the speed of light," I sang. He smiled, and I gave him another nod of encouragement. All of a sudden, I faintly saw Clevis' Santa hat drop to the ground. Gripping to me for dear life, Clevis looked like he's about to fall off a steep cliff. Clevis thrust his way on my back, and I held firmly but it was too much to handle. I didn't want to get hurt, but I let him descend, off his imaginary rock. Clevis twisted his knee, then his shin, and finally his ankle. He shrieked with agony, and looked as though he's about to cry. He put his bare hand against the ice and tried to push himself up, but his ankle twirled even more. I called Coraline over. We pulled him up together, and Coraline took him to the wall.

On our way back to the buses, I trudged with Coraline. We didn't talk too much after, neither did Clevis and I. I skated around for a bit. I watched everyone improve little by little. I viewed the smile on their faces when they slid a few strides. The professional skaters whirled around the rink, not caring of their surroundings. The rowdy boys raced against each other, and knocked one another in the process. I saw the disappointment in The Wolves after I let Clevis go, for the second time. I wanted the strength to hold him up to the sky, to carry him on my back, to assist without hurting him. I wanted to help him reach for the stars, but I couldn't. Clevis and Coraline left me on the ice, again.

"For you information Minnie... you never told me about you and Clevis being together. I just heard it as a rumor, so, why do you think you couldn't tell me in person?" Coraline questioned. I punted a pebble in the parking lot. "Because I didn't want you to kill me."

If I told Coraline I'm dating her enemy, she'd murder me, quite literally since she doesn't own the cleanest record. I kicked another pebble. That tiny little rock is myself, and Coraline is a shoe about to crush me. "Well, that is true."

She didn't do anything after except giggle, "No worries! I'll accept this, only because we're friends," For once, I agreed with her. Friends... I like that.

"Coraline, I'm as culpable as a guilty person can be. I think it'll be best if I apologize to Clevis when we arrive back at school," I noted. She nodded her head.

"I want to see him now...," I wished, staring at his full bus.

"Let's GO. Quickly. Nobody will notice if you're on the other bus," Coraline breathed, looking around. We scrambled to the steps and I plopped down next to where Clevis is sitting. He stared out the window, not noticing I'm here. I am here, and I always will be.

"Clevis, I'm sorry for not helping you up. I am here now, and I always will be," I surmised. I spoke my mind, and the truth.

"Really?" He asked, staring off into space.

I nodded my head.

"I love you Minnie." Well, I would kiss him on the spot, but this wouldn't be school appropriate.

Chapter 4

It is awe-inspiring of how a person who was once a stranger weeks ago, can suddenly mean the world to you. Love, is what Clevis said. "I love you Minnie," is what he said. Love, a variety of different emotional and mental states, typically ranging from the deepest interpersonal affection to the simplest pleasure, as Google says. The love as in, one of the most influential words on our planet. Back in the 1900s, saying you love someone is a rare moment, but now, Clevis said it at the age of fourteen. That signifies a change in this generation, people don't call it the four-lettered-L-word, but Clevis... he said it with zero hesitation.

That unexpected word stranded with me all through Winter Break, like myself on a desert, where sand is blowing into my eyes. The tiny grains of love are floating around, making me weaker with each day passing. I'm prepared to ride on a three humped camel if such a thing exists. Even though my thoughts are in a burning temperature, Winter Break was cold. My mind is in a harsh, frigid, blizzard, with no snow angels to save my soul. Despite the freezing storm destroying my inner electricity, my flashlight batteries are still in sight.

A new light entered for the year of 2017, because this is the time I'll fulfill my New Year's resolution. Most people never keep their resolutions, and take myself for instance, I never follow through with them. I try something, like staying more organized, or doing my homework every night. I would be strong for a week, than collapse like a tired worker working in a retail shop on a Monday. This year though, I'll keep Clevis in my pocket, and pretend he's a wallet full of cash. Despite the drama, my resolution is to date Clevis for a long period of time. I'll follow through like hitting a baseball. In fact, I'll hit a home run, out of the park, out of the country with the excitement I held. I will progress as a Wolf, as a girlfriend, as a person, and after I win the Center Middle School annual geography bee, I'll whack the ball out of the world.

Geography is the study of physical features of the earth and its atmosphere. Of human activity as it affects and is affected by these, including the distribution of populations and resources, land use, and industries. When Mrs. Short announced it, I slapped my knee, screamed with glee, and my brain grew like a geographic tree.

The next day, I trudged to science with my face buried in the World Encyclopedia. I struggled to bring the sagging book through the door. My arms strained with pain as I took a seat in the front row. At least there is no seating chart, because we are starting to learn about galaxies and the distance between them. Either that, or Mrs. Moon got some sense knocked into her.

"Overachieving again Minnie? Wait, of course you're studying, you're a dweeb."

Taking that comment to no offense, I rolled my eyes and held up the book.

"Actually Victoria, if you read the cover of this two foot book, than you would've figured out I'm going to be participating in the geography bee. In here, there are maps of every country, regions, and it is a geographers dream," I happily explained. "However, this should be hard because there will be loads of competition, and intimidating questions, so I'll be studying 24/7."

"I want to do it!" Clevis exclaimed, jumping up and down like an ecstatic rabbit. I'm holding out poisonous carrots, and he's trying to bite them, as always. Victoria shrieked with laughter.

"Are you sure Clevis? We are going to be against each other," I cautioned. Victoria clapped her hands with pure joy, like a toddler is jumping on the trampoline. She's basically a Kardashian, the perfect metaphor to describe a wolf like her.

"Clevis, you HAVE to do it! If 'The Couple of the Year' is going to be there, than The Wolves will be there to cheer you on!" Victoria said. I can imagine The Wolves eating popcorn and making dramatic expressions as if they went to the Grammys or Golden Globes awards show. "Clevis, listen to me. There are a lot of intelligent people entering this competition..."

"We can study together at my house! And... wait for it, wait for it... WE CAN PLAY IN THE SNOW!!!" He waved his arms to make air angels. "Play: an activity engaged in for enjoyment and recreation, especially by children," defined by the Google Dictionary. I'm glaring at the word, 'children'. If this is a definition of common words bee, I'll definitely win. I'm not very excited to 'play' in the snow, but I still accepted his offer to study at his house.

"Awesome! My mommy will text your mommy to remind her about bringing a snowsuit, for PLAYING in the snow."

Play... that word again, and he says it so willingly... like love...

As Dorothy would say, "There is no place like home." Clevis' house is a mess, and I'm not sure how I would survive here. Over the past few weeks, I imagined what his house would look like. I never expected for the walls to be covered with original paintings, or for the shelves to be filled with heirlooms. There are vases, ancient library books, and a creaky wooden floor, but in the middle of a living room is a statue of what looks like his great grandfather. Clevis is the clumsy type of person to break antiques.

I waved goodbye to my mom, and she smirked. A mother proud of her daughter getting a boyfriend with a cultural house, but only if she looked into this more... I carried my sagging duffel bag, which is filled with a hideous hat, minuscule mittens, a scratchy scarf, bothering boots, and my disastrous dignity, about to be embarrassed to death by playing in the snow. This is supposed to be a significant study session, in fact, I had a glorious vision of us making geography flashcards, than laughing about the towns with swear words in it.

I dropped the bag on the stained rug in Clevis' room. The room is light blue, with gigantic airplane wall stickers, with faces on the planes. On his desk, are stick people drawings, picture books, Legos, and stuffed animals on the twin sized bed. He must be showing me his brothers room, so I prepared to travel to the next destination. Clevis jumped on the bed. I don't think this is his younger siblings room.

"Seeing as though we're in your room, let's start our sturdy study session," I claimed. I rummaged through my bag. "Hold on, my World Encyclopedia should be in here... somewhere." I continued to search for my laptop. Hello? Hard and cold surface book surface? Where are you?! As soon as I realized it, I whispered the towns with swears to myself. I forgot my only ticket to this study session.

"Well Clevis, I guess we can't study for the geography bee that is in five short days. 120 little hours. 7,200 small minutes. 432,000 tiny seconds.

"Let's talk about our first kiss," he speculated. The complete opposite topic of geography is kissing. "I brought a list of questions about it!"

A list of questions? That is a considerable question. Clevis grabbed a paper out of his drawer and sat down. He smirked and unfolded it and there is writing until the very end of the page. He left the drawer open, and in there, hundreds of letters I spotted, from Clevis' former crush, Jillian. Seeing as though I pay attention to his hand writing in class, these must of been from awhile ago. Jill is newly apart of The Wolves, and the only reason why she qualifies is because she's appealing, with her long black hair, and radiant gray eyes. She is also one of the smartest people, it shows with her name on the wall as 'junior valedictorian'. A few years back, when we had our first dance in sixth grade, Clevis asked her to go with him, and feeling bad for him, she said yes. At the dance, Jill completely ignored him, and left Clevis sobbing in the center of the dance floor. Her fierce smile may symbolize the light in the Arctic Circle, but really, there is a fire there.

"About our kiss, should we do it inside or outside? How hard should it be? Can I tell my parents about it? How about the angle? What kind of breath mint should I take before it? Can I please tell my parents? Perhaps we should try to make it long? We should beat a school record!" Clevis widely suggested. One thing that glued itself to my mind is the fact Clevis is keeping letters from Jill. I stared at them from where I'm sitting, and now I'm creating my own list of questions.

"Clevis, I brought a list of questions for you too."I took out a blank piece of paper from my pocket. I held it up to my face.

"First, what's in your second drawer to your right?"

"Why are there several letters from Jill, your former crush?" I coaxed with more serious suspicion. I imitated Clevis by scratching my chin, such as a detective trying to find an answer. He waited, and blushed, blocking the papers.

"Final question. Why the hesitation Clevis Cleveland?"

He puckered his lips and took out several papers from the drawer. He handed them to me, shaking. I read the one lying at the bottom of the pile. "Dear Clevis, meet me after the last bell, trust me, from Jill," is what it said. I gave it back to Clevis, and he had about ten letters in his hand, and he claimed more from other drawers. He held these keepsakes for the longest time. They are a treasure to him.

"Minnie, please rip these. I love you, and not Jill. I am over her."

Clevis teared the first one. My paper heart got taped back together, and I ripped away my fears and frights in the world. Clevis ripped another, creating confetti of his former crush. The tiny scraps of snow-flakes falling, making myself as joyful as the time it first snowed in the science room. I ripped some with style. I ripped up the thing holding me behind. I snatched them, and made them into a recycled collage.

"Minnie, let's go play in the snow!!"

I groaned, and longed to stay in the snow I made. I'm the cloud birthing the snowflakes in his room, or the God who controls when the snowflakes are slushy or satisfying. I left the tiny fragments of paper, and trudged into the cold world.

Clevis took sleds out of the garage, and I huffed and puffed as I tried to catch up to him in my snowsuit. It has been years since I was in this thing.

"Where are the hills?" I asked. Without answering, Clevis climbed the piles of ice the snow plow made, the 90 degree angle ones. The 'hill' is so small, my feet could be touching the ground, and I could touch the top of it.

Unlike myself, Clevis screamed with delight while pushing down, causing the neighbors to peek out their windows. He kept on 'sledding' and 'playing'. Clevis a three humped camel born with wings to fly. He is flying backwards into his childhood, or perhaps he never left it. I pre-tended to be happy and cheerful, but I desire for him to be a little more mature about it.

"Clevis, I'm getting bored. Can we just take a walk or something else?" I asked. He refused and continued to sled. "I want to do all these hills. This is a big one!" He piped, pointing to a six foot pyramid of ice. I crossed my arms and grunted, like a horse without his hay, or carrots, or without a decent reputation.

As we finished, I didn't like it how Clevis is not only embarrassing himself, but me too. I tried to keep these doubtful thoughts away, but they kept hitting my brain, giving me a concussion, or like a percussion banging in my mind. A voice starting whispering to myself, 'no', but I ignored it.

Clevis and I hiked into his backyard. Trees covered the road and I sensed prickers beneath the snow. Snow and frost shielded the branches, and the birds are flying from trees to branch, getting whisked away in the wind. The clouds followed a color pattern of yellow, pink, orange, red, purple, blue, dark, and black. Behind me is the sun, and I gazed towards the moon in the horizon. Clevis gazed over my mouth, wanting a kiss... making it quite obvious.

We stood there together in silence, listening to life around us. I mean, this is the exact setting, the precise time, the accurate world, the faithful life... but the correct boy?

I imagined us in the clouds, miles away from The Wolves, the science classroom, the seating chart. I visualized the moon reflecting on us in the night sky. The snow quietly falling on our heads, us holding hands. One thing that transcends time is the feeling of wind sweeping you off your feet, and traveling through open space. Our love traveled through the solar system, similar to a shining shooting star. I soothed the warmth of the sun, the life of Earth, the grand size of Jupiter. I wore the rings of Saturn, and swam in the waves of Neptune. I blushed the color of Mars, but froze in the frigid temperature in Uranus. I stood at the height of Venus, and longed to be the roman god of Mercury. I held the Milky Way galaxy in my clammy palms. I'm no longer in a geographic place, but where am I exactly? In the middle of life, with Clevis, the person whom I love. My spirit owl flied in a circle above us, and indeed, her tiny little orange feather showed. Many uncertainties took over this night, many questions, but for the fact, I felt like I am loved.

I brought my lips closer to his, and I was soon thanking the gods of love. Actually, I'm not really being grateful for the gods of love. I am sometimes wondering if he even deserves this, earns the person who I really am. Indeed, a list of questions is what I have, because I don't think I am feeling the love tonight.

Today is tonight, and tonight is today. The present, not the past, nor the future. I peered out the window to reveal solid blackness. No moon, no stars, no spaceships or planes. Nothing, only the black matter space holds. The night sky is a base coat of dark black paint, so simple, yet, its darkness to it overpowered. The night is my heart right now, from the regrets of wasting my first kiss on a child. I regretted every act I pursued, even the action of myself being born. I am buried underground, with grass growing over my feet. It will suffocate me, then a red rose with prickers will grow. I pricked my finger on the spindle of a spinning wheel, and now I wanted to sleep for a hundred years.

Today is tonight, and tonight is today. The present, not the past, nor the future. I marched into the geography bee, and only about fifty people showed up. The cafeteria is set up so the tables turned into benches, and the stage had fifteen seats, facing the audience. A podium stood right in the center, and Mrs. Short is there, taking attendance.

The Wolves are huddled in a circle, all whispering. Victoria followed her word, and brought The Wolves to cheer us on. I clapped my hands and joined them, jumping up and down inside.

"WHERE is Clevis?" Victoria demanded, stomping her foot.

"He can't make it," I croaked. My black heart beating louder, so loud it could make someone go deaf. I gritted my teeth. By the time I reach age thirty, they will be all chipped away from all the gritting I'm doing. The Wolves whimpered, and sat down disappointed.

"Girls, if Clevis isn't coming, than Jill and I will sign up," Victoria declared. I glared over at Jill, and she looked like she returned from a fashion show. She wore a dress with crystals and blue roses in every corner, and her hair flowed down to her knees. I'm wondering why she isn't in an academically gifted school yet, where all the rich kids go and become models.

Jill stood up with Victoria, and they went to sign up. Victoria is probably doing it so she can get attention, and Jill is undertaking it because Victoria wants her too. They came back two minutes before the geography bee started. Name tags are attached to Victoria's expensive jean jacket, and Jill's practical wedding dress. I fastened mine to my middle class t-shirt. Jill and Victoria sat right and left of me, and we are ready to begin with our fourteen other competitors.

Sorry, I meant to say fifteen, seeing as though Clevis bolted through the door beating the clock striking 7:00. "HEY MINNIE!! TURNS OUT, MY DAD COULD GIVE ME A RIDE!! NOW, YOU CAN BEAT ME, ONCE AND FOR ALL!!!! THAN AFTER THIS, WE CAN KISS AGAIN!!!" Clevis shouted across the room. Well... that is one way to make an entrance.

"Minnie!! Minnie!! WHERE CAN I SIT?!?!"

I buried my face in shame and embarrassment. For once, I am not inwardly enjoying it. Jill and Victoria are cracking up, on either side of me. The audience is glaring at him, than at me, than at him again. We are in the center of attention, of course we are. A circus came here tonight. I'm the man on the tightrope, about to fall off. Clevis is the brave and courageous lion, getting everybody to stare at him like he's insane.

Clevis kicked his legs up and down, after sitting next to me. He's more energetic than usual, if this is possible. He attached his name tag to his blue button down shirt. He wore his cliched Nike pants. What I mean by cliche is, he wears those same pants everyday. Every single day. Does he ever wash them? Probably in the middle of the night. Do you want to know how I know this mysterious case? It is noticeable.

After greeting everyone, Mrs. Short strided up to the podium. She got everyone's attention, it was quite easy though, considering Clevis got everybody's attention for her already.

"First off, take a deep breath! This can be stressful to the people who are afraid to participate in class, or who are shy in general. Do take a breather," Mrs. Short spoke. "There will be three rounds. Twenty questions for each round and the questions will become harder as it goes on. It could go from multiple choice to fill in the blank answers, and so forth. After 10 questions, we'll keep the top ten to continue from there. So good luck, and do your best," Mrs. Short finished. There is a quiet and slow applause. Mr. Cleveland gave a standing ovation, being the loudest of them all. Now I can see why him and Clevis are related. Like father like son. My dad peered at him, then gave me a glare. This is my dad's first time seeing Clevis in person.

Despite that, I am here to win. Clevis will not distract me from my goal because I studied all week, and I cannot be more confident. I know the highest point on Earth, the deepest ocean, the most ancient landmarks. Mountains, deserts, and the scariest caves also. I respired the world's freshest air, and froze as cold as the tip of Antarctica. I was as deep as the lowest abyss, but as tall as the atmosphere.

"Alright! This concludes our first round. As we head into the second, there will be only ten participants, and we will eliminate one by one. For now, you may go back to your seats while we prepare," Mrs. Short spoke. "One question, one person gone."

As soon as my name got called, I clapped my hands with pure joy. I am close to reaching my goal, and after winning this, I will be the wolf on the peak of the rock. I sat while Jill, Victoria, and Clevis gave me a thumbs up.

We all got whiteboards and dry erase markers. I'm prepared to win, and to celebrate with Clevis. We would go out to dinner, ask for a table for two, roses in a vase between the two of us. Our parents would sit on the other side of the restaurant, not eavesdropping on our conversations. We'll talk and chuckle all night, flirting with each other. But for the way Clevis is, that won't be a reality. When I glanced at the crowd again, Clevis is walking out the door with Mr. Cleveland, and Jill. They're both laughing, and leaving me to fight for my own. With that, the other Wolves are snickering. In the snap of a finger. He just... left.

I got the first question wrong. I definitely knew where Niagara Falls is, but this moment, I didn't know anything. No landmarks, no oceans, nothing. I didn't know the place I am in.

"I'm sorry Minnie, but you are eliminated. You may now take a seat and watch and the rest, or enjoy your night," Mrs. Short said. The audience clapped one last time for me. I didn't even pay attention. I blankly stood up, and left the premises.

"You did well Minnie. At least you got into the top ten! I'm proud of you," my dad congratulated me. We're in the car going back home, and the sky is darker than before. I smiled at his comment. "What did you think of Clevis? He was pretty excited to give you his first impression. So tell me, did he give you a suitable first impression?" I interrogated. I asked a question, but I'm more hoping for some relationship advice. The one thing he asked me in reply... it kept me up all night.

"Do you love Clevis?" he wondered. At that moment, I hesitated.

"When you love a person, you want them in your life forever. For example, would you wake up one morning and stop loving me? Think about it," my dad explained. He turned away, and I gazed out the window. Another definition of geography is knowing what place you are in. The culture of your town, the landscape you live in, and what mental state you are in. Where have I gone.

Do I love Clevis?

I banged my head on the glass.

I looked at the reflection of myself in my locker while getting my coat. There is a light shade of black outlining my eyes. My eyes had shadows in them, and I had wrinkles, like a stressed, overworking adult. I tossed and turned all night. Do you love Clevis? I can't answer without hurting somebody. It has been twenty seven days since my New Year's resolution to keep Clevis was promised, and now, this is the result of it.

I'm thinking about a break up with him. Nobody keeps their resolutions. A relationship is a two way street, but a five way street is a better saying. A five way street with an intersection with tons of stoplights. Clevis and I are too young for couples therapy, and I'm not sure if he notices a break up at stake.

"Minnie, any decisions yet?!" Aneska nagged. I opened up to her because I need as much advice as possible. The Wolves and I became friends only because Victoria is my third wheel. I sat at The Wolves lunch table, and hung out with them after school. They are always asking me for daily updates on Clevis, and laughing at it after. Even though it makes me regretful sometimes, that is the price you pay for being in the main group.

Victoria adores me and Clevis' relationship, and for this matter, everybody admires our relationship. Almost everyone would want us to stay together, but me? No. My thoughts went back and forth on this. Now, I wanted freedom. Freedom from drama. Freedom from anything in the world. A huge weight would lift off my shoulders. The freedom. How his heart could be broken. Oh, the freedom. My popular reputation. Still, the freedom. Our love. Freedom. I walked away from my locker with Aneska, looking worse than before.

"I don't know Aneska," I said, walking into my last period class.

"Folks! It is fifty degrees out! Bring your sunglasses because we are going outside on this BEAUTIFUL day!" Mrs. Short exclaimed. Even though Spring hasn't reached us yet, I feel as though I live in an eternal winter. This winter brought no unique snowflakes, or alluring sights. The type of winter which makes you cold, dreary, and the kind which wants you to sigh.

As I slumped outside, I spotted Coraline. I haven't talked to her in such a long time, ever since The Wolves took me in for training. Coraline sat alone in the back row from time to time, looking as glum as ever. She sits by oneself at lunch, and eventually stopped talking to me. She walked to the entrance for outside. I put my hand on her shoulder and spun her around.

"Coraline, I'm sorry I am a selfish, and an over obsessive person. I am aware I'm ignoring you, but I miss you too. I don't want our friendship to end. You're the girl on the right of the seating chart, and that is an important role in my life."

She wrapped her arms around me. "Aw, I missed you to!"

One out of a million problems are solved.

"Minnie, I heard about your relationship problem. Aneska told me,"

Coraline addressed strictly. "I'm not sure if anyone else said this to you already, but listen to your heart. Do what you want to do," Coraline advised. "If you love Clevis, there shouldn't be a hesitation. Love... a state of deep admiration and passion. Liking a person isn't the same as loving them. You should learn to put yourself before others, mainly when The Wolves are caught up in this. Besides, being as single as a pringle is much better," She ended. I took her words seriously.

"My heart is saying no, but my brain is telling me yes," I panted in reply.

"In romantic novels, brains are overrated," Coraline said.

"You read a book?!"

"No, of course not. I watched the movie. Who do you think I am?"

"I will break up with Clevis, at his locker, right after the bell, so I could give him the weekend to cool down," I proclaimed. Coraline smiled, not only because she hates Clevis, but because it is right for me. This break up will be a new chapter of my life, after the time period of the seating chart. He isn't impacting my life in a good way. I also realized throwing away my dream of having love is what's at stake. Sometimes, nightmares can impact us, and they can change for the better. Nightmares about this scared me, but now, it seems like a dream come true.

"That unconventional seating chart," I growled to Coraline. I waved at a tiny snowy owl who I imagined fly above me. The little orange feather gleamed in the sunlight.

I breathed in a cool breeze. I let out one of the biggest deep breaths.

"I'm doing it," I said to myself.

And then... the bell rings. The time has come. A new chapter of my life story is going to be a page turner. I clench my fists and go to his locker. In the hallway, a crowd of people formed around Clevis' locker. All of the popular people in our school, with Victoria in the middle.

Aneska probably texted Victoria about this. As I came into the separate realm, everybody's silent, like the ghost in the back of the science room. Clevis is ghost white at his locker. He knew what's coming. I took a deep breath, like I am going underwater. Everyone is still, like the rocks in the cavernous ocean.

This is the abyss I am talking about. When you fall into a dark hole of drama and can never swim out. This is where I fell, and this is where I will keep falling, no matter what. I thought of the tiny owl I kept seeing. At the windows, looking into my bright blue eyes. Gazing into my life, a spirit from heaven, or a symbolization of my life. Who knows. Nobody knows. Nobody knows anything.

"Clevis, we should break up," I finished. Tears formed beneath his glasses.

All I know is I am in the middle. The middle of a seating chart? No. I am in the middle of everything but a seating chart.

Chapter 5

The sunset drained the sky's bright colors, and from light to dark the sky changed. A lonely night, with black in the atmosphere, no stars shined. The moon took the spotlight, like how I stand out among the rest of life. A new side to breaking up with someone has taken over me. I started a new chapter in my life story, but I am once again, a lone wolf. Howling at the moon, hanging over the horizon.

Eight hours ago, on my own two feet, I stood inside a circle of popular kids hooting and hollering. I wish at that moment, those kids could step into my shoes. Right now, they aren't comfy shoes. They are those kinds of shoes that give you blisters if you walk too far. But there I was, looking at Clevis mournfully, hands clenched, standing like a fallen warrior. I had the urge to run away, to break out of this circle, to bolt wildly and to never come back. To never do what I did.

What am I doing? Answering texts. I got called the 'f'and the 's', word a lot, and I can't say I'm not those words.

I received a text from Victoria... making me collapse.

"Minnie, I cannot believe you dumped Clevis. He was CRYING on the bus. He confided in me. He thought you were the one. 'The one'... HIS TRUE LOVE. Now he's calling himself a jerk. He isn't the bad guy, YOU are. He did nothing wrong, and he's blaming himself for it.

You broke up with him in front of everyone... I'm disgusted. You should go to hell for this. Do you deserve to live Minnie? Do you?"

Victoria is the person who set up this catastrophe. She is the one who smirked the whole time, like a creepy clown stalking your Instagram page. But now, I can only blame myself, Minnie Ann Stickley-Adotte. She's right, I shouldn't go to heaven. I won't walk the golden stairway, or survive in the clouds after I die... and back on Earth, a gardener won't plant a dandelion next to my gravestone. When I told myself I wanted a change in my life, I expected for this to be a fitting change, to make this into my perfect life.

As the clock struck 12:00, Clevis texted me, which I never thought would happen.

"You are right. I am immature, I'm a loser, and I never deserved you to begin with. But... I thought we had something. Something, like love. I loved you, but I guess you didn't like me back."

My heart is broken, like a tear in the wallpaper of life. I finally placed my phone away on the nightstand, and stared at the full moon. That moon out shined the sky, the atmosphere, my world. It stood still. I wonder if Clevis is gazing over the moon. If he's at his window, crying, like myself. Water rolled down my cheeks and my face burned from the heat of sorrow. I hugged my pillow and let the pain soak in. It was at the moment, I wanted Clevis to wrap his arms around me like a blanket. To whisper that everything will be okay. Thinking about this made me sob harder. My vision blurred.

As Mrs. Moon once said, there wouldn't be stars without stardust, just like how there wouldn't be a journey without the seating chart. I sniffled, and the memories of us returned to me. As the timeline went on, I got darker, until there are no bright lights in the sky, and until I did what I did.

In the black night atmosphere, a snowy owl flew to my window.

I opened it to let a cool breeze in. Her eyes twinkled, as she perched herself. Gusts of wind blew, drying my tears, my pains, and fears. "Ah, Minnie... I left a light on for you," The owl voiced calmly. No sound came out, only thoughts, and images. I fell asleep with full moonlight shining upon me. It is quite strange though. Seeing there isn't a moon scheduled for tonight.

I slept for fifteen hours the next day, maybe even more. Here I am, in my bed, the sun is out, blinding my eyes. When I recalled what happened the previous night, I kicked myself in the calf. When I remembered my promise at the beginning of the school year, I booted it again. In September, I said I will focus on my grades and increase my artistic ability. I would impress my teachers, eventually getting a scholarship to a convenient private institution. I told myself I will avoid drama at all costs. Ever since December 2nd, I have done the opposite.

How do I usually make things better? Apologize and move on. If I did something wrong, than I would be punished. Maybe if I apologized, than my punishment would be shorter. If I say sorry to Clevis, than maybe we can move on with our lives. We could possibly be friends, like how the Beatles banded together to create the most foremost and influential group. Clevis and I could make a band and play through this. We can play out the drama, and sing a song perhaps.

"Hi Clevis, listen, I'm sorry about what happened yesterday. It was wrong of me to dump you in front of almost the whole school, and The Wolves. I'm hoping we can be friends. You are a much better friend than boyfriend. I adore your personality, that is how I fell in love with you in the first place. Let's just be friends," I sent to him. Right after I hit send, I realized I said the exact sentence Rogelio texted me when I told him I liked him. "Let's just be friends," is what he said.

Rogelio had me on Cloud 9 ever since we first met in sixth grade. He is Italian, with a tint of Spanish. He may as well be a worldwide superstar, or an American Actor, like Jim Carrey or Tom Cruise. Rogelio's leafy green eyes are magnificent, matching his pearly whites. He is my knight in shining armor, riding on a stallion, waiting to pick me up and bring me to his next Broadway show. Sixth grade homeroom... that was simply wonderful.

It all started when Rogelio noticed me buying lunch in the cafeteria. He says, "HEY Minnie!!," and indeed, that was the catalyst to my overthinking and inferences about him. On Fridays, we would go outside to walk around the track. He told me about his social problems and opened up to me. I gave him good advice on what to do, but, I was thinking to myself whether he liked me back or not. Finally, in the middle of April that same year, I called and said I had a crush on him. That night, and I will never forget it, he said he was maintaining a long distance relationship. He eventually broke up with her, telling me at the dance in seventh grade.

I started stirring up drama, trying to get him to like me back. I asked other people to ask him out for me, and I sent him notes, text messages, and I tried hinting it with him. It was at a school dance when I asked him to dance with me.

"Rogelio, can I dance with you?" I asked. I remember the awkward look on his face, and the desperate look on my face.

"Minnie, NO! I told you this several times, but I don't like you back. We are only friends," he said, walking away. I went home crying. Usually, he says that over text or written on a paper, but he told me with full emotion, and he told the dreadful truth that night. I realized he'd never feel the same way. It was a life lesson I realized the hard way. I learned it over and over again, but to this day, we are still friends. He waves at me in the hallways, and sits next to me sometimes. We talk, we wave, but we are friends, and only friends. We're like two trees growing next to each other. As we moved through the grades together, I would try being closer to him, but his leaves died. We will never be more than friends. It took me a long time to get over Rogelio... so I wonder how long it will take Clevis to get over me.

Clevis never texted back.

Over the next week, the text messages and rude comments decreased in quality and quantity. Fortunately, Clevis got the flu, or perhaps he is sick of all the drama, so he started not feel well for real. Since he isn't here, The Wolves didn't bother me, thank goodness. I'm glad I gave Clevis a few days to cool down, but now, I am sitting at my desk in my room, anxiously waiting for tomorrow.

Another Sunday night is the present, and Clevis is bound to return to school tomorrow. It has been a week and two days since the break up, so anything can happen if he returns. He could scream his lungs out at me in science, or, pour milk on my head at lunch, or, the whole class could be pressuring me. He could get The Wolves to do something nasty, and they would do anything to bring us back together. Speaking of Victoria and The Wolves, I got kicked out of the group. I am the Charlie Brown failing to kick the football during the Peanuts Thanksgiving Special. Victoria is Lucy, the mean and bratty kid. Overall, they ignored me, and I started talking to Coraline again. We sat together at lunch and talked about drama, the drama club, and drama outside of school, and anything drama related. To talk to somebody who won't judge you when you're constantly getting judged is very nice in the worst of times. I laid down in my bed, and loathed what could happen the next day. All of a sudden, my phone rang. I reached my hand over and picked it up from the nightstand. I answered with a mournful voice.

"Hi Coraline, how's---"

"Min, Twitter, NOW."

She hung up. Well, when I first read it, I stopped breathing. I gazed over it over and over again and each time I peruse it, it only got defective. I have a stomach ache. Something was bound to happen, I just didn't know it would be today, tonight. I sank on my bed covers, and dread spilled over me like black paint on a white masterpiece. I picked up my phone again, stared at the devil. This is turning into an addictive drug. As I read it again, tears froze in my eyes from the chills down my spine. I tossed and turned all night, for the tenth time this month.

I despise this science room. Math class is better, and learning about nitty gritty fractions is better than this science classroom. In fact, this is worse than Physical Education, where you run a mile and get graded for it. It is worse than History, where you learn about the battles which don't matter anymore. After stomping into the Science room, I sat in Mrs. Moon's NEW seating chart. The day I got back from the worst weekend of my life, I open the doors to Mrs. Moon assigning new seats. I thought about screaming to her at the top of my lungs, but I saved myself the embarrassment. Coraline is in the front row, AND she put Clevis behind me in the third row. I am in the second row, still in the middle, and still between them.

However, since Clevis' been absent, it has been easier for me because if he is here, then I'm not sure whether he'd be staring at my head, or paying attention to the lesson. In less than seven minutes though, I will be in line for my own funeral.

"Hey Minnie, how's it going?" Mrs. Moon asked, casually typing away on her computer. I slumped down into my desk. This became a routine now, where I come to science early from lunch. Just like when I

first spotted the imaginary snowy owl perched on the window. With my
diverse mood swings, Mrs. Moon would ask me how I am, and I would
answer in a different way. She glanced at me when I didn't respond.

"Are you okay?"

"I heard you broke up with Clevis," she quickly acknowledged. I
nodded my head and uncrossed my arms. She got up from her desk and
sat next to mine, in the second row.

"How are things with him? It must be hard," she murmured. She's
got that right. It's harder than the word, hard. It is tough, if that is a
word surpassing hard. "This is tough," I said. "But, I don't regret a
thing about the break up. What's hard is the pressure of having to face
him today, the pressure of being the most selfish person in school, and
the pressure of having to deal with Clevis' post on Twitter."

"His post?"

I nodded my head and took out my phone. "Yes... he posted something about me last night."

"Can I see it?" She asked. I went to his page, and his profile picture
is a capture of me and him together. I'm surprised he hasn't deleted it
yet. Mrs. Moon read the post out loud.

"Dear Minnie, I miss you more than anything in the world and I
will do anything to bring us back. I still love you more than I love my
brothers. I wish you felt the same. I miss you, I want to love you forever, until our grave days arrive. Again, I love you."

She gripped my phone and made a concerned expression. "You can
read the comments too."

"Clevis, if you show this much admiration and she doesn't appreciate it, that just shows you are the better person,"commented by pretty
and petty Victoria. Victoria is always on social media, finding information on other people, sorting out their weaknesses and using it against
them. That one comment got over five likes.

"Any decision could make or break everything. I hold the power to get back together with him, making The Wolves satisfied. With that move, I won't be happy, or, I could continue to be the biggest selfish jerk in school. Have a difficult reputation for the rest of my life, but to be free to be myself and to do what I want to do."

I stared into Mrs. Moon's dark brown eyes. She leaned back in her chair, and let out a deep breath, like a person being able to breathe on the moon. There she is, breathing all the air. Savoring the oxygen on the rocky surface.

"Minnie, I know this is rough for you, but I want you to stay true to yourself. This is YOUR decision, not anyone else's. You have a sweet personality but you got to learn how to put you before others in a situation like this. My advice to you is you should step away from social media for a few weeks, until things cool down. Turn off your phone and go for a hike! Spend some quality time drawing!" She marveled. Like Coraline said, follow your heart. Except, by following it, that got me to be in this place. I'm running out of oxygen.

"Do you know what Mrs. Moon? I'm going to delete all social media on my phone, for two weeks. It will be an experiment to see how it affects my mental health. Besides, isn't that what science is for? To discover things?"

I looked at the clock, and my heart started racing. I'm going to see Clevis in less then a minute. Mrs. Moon winked and stepped on her imaginary red carpet. Kids are starting to coming through the door. As I waited for Clevis, I felt myself run out of air. He came through the door, and I felt... absolutely nothing.

"Before we start, I need to change around a few seats," Mrs. Moon objected. I perked up, and got excited for a moment. I'm half hoping Clevis didn't see me crossing my fingers.

"Minnie, why don't you move to the empty desk in the front row?

The one in the middle, right between Coraline and Rogelio," she decided, satisfied. I happily got out of my seat and went to the front row. I
no longer despise the science room. I can see an oxygen mask, but in a
further distance, on the dark side of the moon.

Usually, I would rather be in my desk writing on a piece of white
lined paper. I do like school, studying for tests, the excitement of receiv-
ing a good test score, or presenting a presentation about a fun topic. I
like the class activities where we play games, and laugh at each others
comments. However, after this dramatic week, my admiration for this
is the exact opposite. Don't get me wrong, I still like school, but I like
it without The Wolves bugging me and asking questionnaires about the
aftermath of the relationship. Mostly, they are nagging us to get back
together. I keep on saying no, and it's becoming tiring, like when it
rains for five days straight. Flooding is everywhere. A flood of populars.
I can't escape. No boat is in sight. I'm getting rained on. I am soaked.

After Friday though, I'll be home free. I'll run to my house, waving my arms in the air like a maniac, then slumping on my couch and
watching sitcoms. But first, I have to live through that nightmare, which
will be as painful as any Monday. Today is not going to be a fine day.
Science is first period and if I can make it through this, and lunch, than
I will be clear for home plate. As I walked in, the desks are set up like
a theater. No seating chart! Clevis is in the back with The Wolves so I
quickly moved past them. As I sat alone in the front row, Mrs. Moon
glided the red carpet, singing.

"Mercury is the closest planet to the sun, it is small and done.
Venus comes next, the hottest one, but not perplexed. Earth is the only
life, and not one knife. Mars holds the biggest canyon, with companion.

The gassy planet of Jupiter, the largest you will find, but not stupider. Saturn's rings around the outside, gliding to classroom insides. Uranus is funny 'cause it spins and is punny. Neptune looks blue, the coldest of its kind too. Pluto doesn't exist," Mrs. Moon sang, pointing to all the planets hung on the ceiling. Everybody stared at her, like she was breaking out into a song.

"I know it may seem like a lot, but it is only a paragraph. We are going to memorize it by singing. An old and classic children's video," she bubbled. In elementary school, we relished vocalizing our hearts out. I hated fourth grade chorus though, because it was the most boring class. But we were forced to sing, and now, in eighth grade, nobody will sing or say a word, no matter what the consequence is. This is called torture, says the person who croaks words when trying to sing. The class groaned when hearing this news.

At first, we had to sing it as loud as possible, than people got to sing it in groups. That video somehow exaggerated it, because the song had low going straight to high notes, long and short also. My voice would sound like a knuckle cracking. I'm not participating, no matter what.

"Do it with Clevis. Sing it together," Victoria demanded, sitting in the seat next to me.

"No," I answered. There is no way I'm doing this. I couldn't even audition for Frozen from being so embarrassed.

"Please?"

"Nope, not happening."

I thought of Mrs. Moon's words, and how I got to stand up for myself. I glanced at the lyrics, completely ignoring Victoria. In the background, the whole back row is begging me to sing with him. Clevis perked up when he heard his name.

"Alright," Victoria remarked. She snapped her finger and the class immediately quieted down. Everybody's eyes are on Victoria and I. Some people looked at Clevis when hearing my name. Victoria casually strolled around my desk. "How about a deal then Min? If you do a duo with Clevis, than I will do a solo," She offered. She slammed both hands on my face.

"Do it," She sneered, waiting for my answer.

The only reason why I'm hesitating is because of what happened in October. We did an activity similar to this, but we had to sing a cheesy song about gases in space. Victoria was forced to sing by the other Wolves, and she was horrifying. I never laughed harder, in fact, I fell out of my seat with laughter controlling my body. If she can embarrass herself again, and if The Wolves are satisfied after this, and if they stop bothering Clevis and I, than that is a classic two birds with one stone scenario. I'm throwing stones at Victoria and The Wolves, fighting back for my rights. Putting myself first, and this might be the way.

"Fine."

Clevis stood up and clapped his hands. Victoria smirked.

"You first," I implied. She nodded and went to the center of the room. She had this confident look on her face, which made me chuckle. She's pretty, rich, popular, but one thing she isn't good at is singing. I will enjoy this as much as I loved watching animal fails online.

Something I couldn't expect in a million years is Victoria being extraordinary. When she started, she sang beautifully. Like a soft feather hitting the grass, or a delicate angel yelling. She paused before the chorus, and broke out in full symphony. She hit the high notes higher, and the low ones lower. We're at a concert and she had a microphone in her hand, singing her heart out. I am impressed, and boiling up with anger. This is not the deal I made. The trade isn't embarrassment for amazement. It is embarrassment for embarrassment. If I would've known, I wouldn't agree to this in a million years.

"Pluto doesn't exist..." she fairly ended. Everyone applauded and she pretended to drop the imaginary microphone, whipping her hair. "Your turn Minnie. I hope you do as well as myself," she scolded. She is the worst.

I took Victoria's place in the center of the room, facing the front board with the lyrics. I gulped as Clevis stands up on his tippy-toes. He stood next to me, and also swallowed, like a fish, swimming in circles of trouble.

"Minnie, are you sure you're okay doing this?" Mrs. Moon questioned. I nodded my head. Well, in about five seconds, I'll take a huge downfall on my life, once again, as if I haven't taken enough.

Mrs. Moon began the music and I croaked the words. I am the opposite of a symphony, in fact, I'm a reverse of the best singer. As the worst vocalist in the world, I sang in a crooked whisper, bringing my hands to cover my face. When the high note came, I went from a mumble to a full blown out scream, like the loudest cowbell. That certainly made the popular kids in the back row laugh, like I'm the Victoria in October. I finished the song almost choking, which made everyone snicker harder. People can be cruel, (The Wolves). As for Clevis... he ended up sitting in the corner, bailing for the whole thing. Isn't this supposed to be a duo? It was a solo to me... a disastrous solo.

"Amazing Minnie. If you thought about how I sang in October, well... I had a cold," Victoria sassed. She whipped her hair again. "You and Clevis make the perfect duo, so you should get back together with him," she added. She strolled away, cherishing her victory.

Duo? Duo she says. The bell rang and I ran out of the room. I fought back tears, and dragged myself to second period. People say Fridays are the best day of the week. I disagree.

Well... I'm ready to collapse on my couch, and binge watch a sitcom. I need one which will make me forget everything, and one that will make me crack up, what I didn't see earlier. I'm ready to never go back to school, in fact, I thought about transferring if possible. I'm ready to throw my phone in a river and let the water seep into it. Into all my text messages I got about my future solo singing career, and to wash them away.

After getting kicked out of the group, Coraline invited me to sit at her table for lunch. I accepted the offer the first time, and many times after. Even though sitting with Coraline is a lower class of popularity, it is much more fun. We would talk about science, the inside scoop on the drama, and drama club. Coraline let me vent to her about the pressure that's going on. As much as I love lunch, it gets VERY annoying when Victoria calls me over to their table. I'm always over there for the longest time, answering questions. This has been happening all week.

"Min, don't go over there. Pretend like you're busy, or ignore them for heaven sake!" Coraline would say every time. It's hard to pretend like they don't exist, and so I go back when they called for me. As for today, I'm prepared for the worst. In the hallway, I told Coraline about what happened in Science.

"I'm sorry I wasn't here this morning. I skipped first period, because Science is boring. Don't you want to slap Victoria in the face?"

I would LOVE to slap Victoria in the face. "That wouldn't be school appropriate."

One of Coraline's pet peeves is when I'm a rule follower, and when I say it out loud. This has been like this since the beginning of the year, and I enjoy being like this. It is irritating to other people, like Coraline.

"Minnie! stop being such a goody two shoes! I'm going to start calling you, GTS. For goody two shoes."

For the first time that day, I laughed. "So.. GTS, where should we sit GTS?" She asked. That made me chortle harder, and I haven't cracked up like this all week.

We both sat down, still laughing. Coraline immediately stopped when she glanced behind my head. "GTS, look behind you. Slowly."

I turned to find the popular table, the table right next to us. I turned my head back to Coraline, who panted heavily. They could be eavesdropping.

"Should we change our lunch table before they call me?" I asked her.

"No, we could learn to deal with them."

"Minnie!! Come over here!!" Victoria yowled, frantically waving her hand.

"Ignore..."

"Well, I can't exactly ignore them," I breathed back. They called my name again, slightly louder.

"Ignore..."

"As much as I want to, I can't..." I said.

"Min! Whatever Coraline is saying, don't listen to her! Come over here!" They kept on yelling.

"I have to go over there. They won't stop."

Coraline sighed and let her head fall to the table. I got up and stood at the edge of their table, hiding disappointment. Jill stands up and approaches me.

"Hey Min, I heard about you singing with Clevis during Science. I could've been there, but I had an entrance exam for an Ivy League School. Now, are you sure you don't want to get back together with him? From the videos Vicky took, you two seemed like an ideal duo."

"Hold on... a video? Victoria, please delete that."

She shook her head, and whipped her hair for the third time today. "Nah, I think I'll keep it. Besides, you were absolutely amazing," she denied. Everyone shrieked with laughter, like the hyenas they are.

I looked over at Coraline, who is eavesdropping. She made a G with her hands, a T, then an S. "Well, according to the student handbook of 2017, you may not take photography or film of a peer without their permission," I said. "There could be consequential consequences." Victoria is dumbstruck.

"Goody two shoes," Coraline imitated. Ideas are forming in my head... I smirked while heading to their table again. I'm a lion, ready to conquer The Wolves, and to eat them one by one. I walked over there, smirking.

"I miss you," Clevis confessed. Was he here before? I can imagine Victoria handcuffing him to the table. I can also imagine she used some sort of magical spell to manipulate him to say that. She's using my weaknesses against me, utilizing Clevis as a weapon. I thought of Mrs. Moon's words.

"I want you to stay true to yourself. This is YOUR decision, not anyone else's. You are a sweet person but you got to learn to put yourself before others in a situation like this."

"You are so annoying," Victoria gritted in mental agony.

"Yes, yes I am. Did you know you can abbreviate the 'you are' into 'you're'? It is one syllable less."

She looked like she's about to explode, but Clevis looked like he's going to explode with laughter. "Just... get back together with Clevis. You could make his day, or even make his life," Victoria tried. I uncovered my hand to reveal my math homework. On this sheet, we had to define a ton of terms and definitions. It was tedious work but I knew it could pay off one day.

"Stop being so IRRATIONAL Victoria. Don't waste a FRACTION of my time," I started. I heard groans, but in my mind, I'm laughing my ankles off.

"Please..." Victoria pleaded.

"Do you want Clevis to be staring at my ACUTE angles? When I look at myself in the mirror, I enjoy looking at my precise angles."

Clevis is blushing, but nobody's blushing as hard as Victoria.

"Why all the reddening Vicky? Are you STRAIGHT?"

I held a diagram with a 180 degree line. That got people's attention, and what did the teachers do? Laugh, just like everyone else.

"Oh my (swear) god... YOU, GROSS?!" Victoria screamed.

"This doesn't add up. Are you 90 degrees because you're looking RIGHT!"

The whole cafeteria is hooting and hollering, like they're seeing a fight in an NHL hockey game.

"Get back together with Clevis," Victoria demanded. This is a problem.

"Me? Getting back with my X? I wonder Y..."

"Me and Clevis both agree you should ask him out," she barked. Being in the spotlight can be good and bad. When I was in science, it was horrible, but Victoria got her chance to shine. Now, I have the opportunity of finishing her, like how she finished me.

"Clevis and I," I corrected. Now everyone at that table broke into laughter. Victoria turned into the Victoria trying to sing in October. She glared at Aneska, and pushed herself away from the table, like a dramatic celebrity.

"This isn't over!"

"So... is running away dramatically how you FUNCTION?" I finished.

She stomped out the door on her high heels. That made everyone roar harder. I used my own method to embarrass Victoria, similar to how she embarrassed me before. When Victoria shouted this isn't over, I knew many more battles will come in my way. Perhaps I'll correct her on her pronunciation next time.

Clevis freed himself from the imaginary handcuffs and gave me a high five. As I stared at my weakness, Clevis, it came back to me. My regrets, my pity, the memories, and a tint of love. Valentine's Day is next Tuesday, and I am prepared for the worst. With my appropriate senses and puns, I will not let the pressure come in the way of my happiness.

"GTS!!" Coraline shouted. The Wolves silenced. Nobody else knew what it meant, but I... myself... I smiled with confidence and pride.

Chapter 6

"Hello folks! It is nice to see all your friendly faces again. I know it has been awhile since our last drama club meeting, but now, we are back and in action. I want every person on their tippy toes for the next month and a half, because our show is going to be held on March 30th," Mrs. Short informed.

"I am going to start with the dance number, 'For the First Time in Forever'. I'll need Elsa, Ana, and my dancers. Please place into position, and for the rest of you, don't get into any trouble," Mrs. Short concluded. Victoria is already in center stage, smirking like the devil she is. Ever since she sang like a star in Science last week, Mrs. Short made some last minute changes to the casting. Of course she gets Elsa, the lead role. I laid back in my seat, still cherishing my big win from last Friday.

On that day, I was the queen of the school, and my king is the championship I pursued. The day ended with everybody hearing about it, congratulating me for taking a stand, and the rest of The Wolves were light-hearted to me. I fell in love with victory, and I even made it my Valentine for this year. However, when we returned today, Victoria has only been mean. She attempted to pour water on my head, and she tripped me in Science. In Math, she tried to make a pun, but that failed. For tomorrow, I have full armor stored in my locker, and a world class dictionary. I memorized every word, so I can correct Victoria on her pronunciation. Tomorrow is Valentine's Day, so for me, I'm visiting my grave tomorrow. On the gravestone, the words carved out are, "R.I.P Minnie's love life. 2003-2003." That grave would be gray, it would be dull, and my grave is dead. This day should really be called National Heartbreak Day. Ever since fourth grade, I would look for the perfect boy to crush on. But my options were limited, seeing that most boys in that grade pick their nose and show it to their friends. Besides getting my heartbroken almost every year, my Valentine's Day is pleasant. I love giving every person in the class little valentine cards, with tiny heart shaped lollipops. After we stopped doing this, National Heart Break Day is what I started calling this. The day where most hearts are either broken, cheated on, or, as single as a pringle. That day is tomorrow, so I am prepared for the worst.

All of a sudden, a pair of hands grasped my arms and pulled me out of the cafeteria. I tried my best to not scream. Pink sparkly nails dug into my skin and long blonde hair whipped across my face. Aneska forced me into the hallway, where myself, Aneska and her fellow Wolves stood. They looked at me sternly.

"Hi?" I asked. I pondered. "Can I help you with someth-"

"We need your final decision," Aneska interrupted.

"On what?" I managed to choke out.

"On your break up with Clevis, of course!" She replied excitedly. If I had a dollar for every time somebody mentions me and Clevis' former relationship, than I would be a millionaire. That isn't an exaggeration. I took a reality check, I checked it, and I counted about two million and fifteen thousand times. If I made a tally mark list starting at three o'clock, one hundred lines would have been drawn by the time midnight arises.

"My answer is still no."

I dropped an imaginary microphone and fled the hallway. They called for me again, like the obsessed 'Plastics' they are. Sometimes, I'm like a doormat. Victoria and her crew could wipe their dirt on me, and leave me out in the cold February weather. Being the doormat I am, I gradually strolled back into the hallway.

Jill stepped forward. "Do you miss him at all?"

I miss myself not being taunted 24/7. I shook my head, and apologized for the million and fifteen thousandth time. In the corner of the dim hallway, I watched as a silhouette stirred. Someone is watching, and I knew exactly whose shadow it is.

"Clevis," I snarled. He stepped into the light, but darkness shows on his face. He held his hand out, like I did for him at that one drama club meeting. Love never accepts a defeat, no challenge it can't meet, no place it cannot go. "Please," he told me.

Suddenly, another arm grabbed mine. Look at that, I'm being kidnapped by... black nails digging into my skin and bony hands harrowing even more. "C'mon Min, it's stage time," Coraline saved, as she dragged me away from Clevis. I let her take me away and back into the cafeteria. The Wolves looked disappointed.

"I can't thank you enough Coraline," I said. "No problem GTS," she finished. I chuckled, and sat down in deep relief. I just sank in a pool, and I tried with eager to swim to the top. Coraline is my lifeguard who saved my life, my identity, my dignity, and who rescued me from a dreadful question.

"I NEED THE ENSEMBLE!!!" Mrs. Short yelled. I walked onto stage with Coraline and spent fifteen minutes singing 'Let it Go'. The whole time, I watched the popular group, who are probably forming another plan. They should let it go. They are huddled in a circle, Clevis in the center.

From the stage, I snuck out the back door and into the hallway. I

needed a walk to saunter away from drama, and drama club. The desire
for this stroll lasted as long as time went on, because every single time
I am encountered by a wolf, I am sick to my stomach. I wanted to run
away to California, where people are nicer.

"Minnie!! Wait up!" Jill and Penelope clamored. They both ran
and jumped on either side of me. From what I know, Jill is mentoring
Penelope in the art of popularity. I didn't know a subject on it is real,
it must be a 2017 thing. I can imagine Jill writing full length textbooks
about it, besides, she does know everything.

"So...how are you?" Penelope asked. I am NOT fine.

"I'm... fine," I assured, with suspicion.

"Can you show us where your locker is?" Penelope begged.

The truth is, I wouldn't be surprised if Victoria knew how to drive
at the age of fourteen, and went out to buy flowers that Clevis would
put in my locker. Something suspicious is going on here, and I intend to
follow this. Better yet, perhaps I'll be gifted with chocolate. The delicious chocolate in those golden boxes, with red ribbons. I'm craving
some Lindt Chocolate. Not that chocolate with almonds though. Those
are the worst kind, and I'm not sure how people can stand the crunchy
bite getting in the way of a creamy flow.

"This way!" I motioned them to my locker. I pretended to act dumb
and just point to my locker. What did I expect next? For them to ask me
to open it.

"Can you unlock it?" Jill asked. I could smell those crispy chocolates from here. I opened my locker and inside, my books and binders
are piled on each other. Papers scattered all over the place, and I should
win a Guinness World Record for most unorganized locker.

"Well, it isn't interesting," I muttered. Jill insisted on keeping it
unlocked. Victoria is probably driving her Lamborghini to the chocolate store at this second. The three of us walked back to drama club, my

locker still cracked open. It was at that moment when I realized Victoria isn't allowed to drive. She couldn't buy chocolate. If there isn't chocolate in this little experiment, than I'm going to be so mad at myself.

After arriving back at drama and seeing Clevis and The Wolves going out the door again, I followed. As I walked down the empty hallways, I inspected all directions, for any Wolves who could be crawling around. The Wolves are looking for prey. I'm an insect to them, but an interesting one with two heads. They certainly want to play around before eating me. As I entered the English Language Arts wing, I peeked out from the wall to spot them putting something into my locker.

"HEY!"

I sprinted to them, and immediately, Clevis and Aneska ran in the other direction. Victoria struggled to keep up with them, seeing as though she's wearing high heels. The only person left is Jill.

"I want access to my locker."

"Well, you can't," Jill replied. She wouldn't move, like the British guard in front of the Buckingham Palace. Holy mother of swears and other bad things I don't want to say, what the heck is happening. Penelope caught up with us, and she lead me back to drama. I looked back at Jill, guarding whatever item is in my locker. I told Coraline everything there is to tell.

While explaining to her what happened, I observed Mrs. Short power the snowflake machine, to produce actual snowflakes during a few scenes. I watched the snow gently fall. I wish I'm a real snowflake. Delicately falling with no worries on my mind.

"Min, let's go to your locker," Coraline sputtered. We are fierce snowflakes in a blizzard, dashing to my locker.

"If Clevis did gift you with chocolate, then I call the chocolate with almonds!!" Coraline claimed, almost out of breath. The only chocolate I like is plain and Clevis knew that, so if he did get me almond chocolates, then I won't be very satisfied. "Of course. Everyone knows that I hate them."

I chuckled nervously while putting in the last number. When I pulled it open, someone pushed me on the ground, and slammed the locker. That same person stood right over me.

"Go back to drama Minnie, and don't come back until tomorrow morning."

"You think you're so durable Clevis. Common sense says that if someone is trying to win you back, then they don't push you on the ground. So if you want me to even consider it, I want access to my locker. NOW."

"Go away."

I snarled at my weakness, and walked away. At that moment, I long for Mrs. Moon's words to still be ringing in my head, that I got to stand up for myself. Sometimes, that isn't possible. I ran to the nearest bathroom with Coraline. Once Clevis watched me go inside, he left. I peeked out the door, and he joined Jill. Who knows, perhaps Jill is a mentor for two students.

"He's gone," I whispered to Coraline.

I glanced out the door again. Clevis and Jill are walking back, so I took it as my cue to run straight to my locker, to open it, and find a note from Clevis. Despite all the dirty papers and unorganized books, this message took the spotlight. I recognized this heart shaped sticky letter. Aneska used them to take notes in Science. The outline had dark pink hearts, while the inside is a huge red Cupid. Clevis' messy handwriting is on the light salmon lines. There is no chocolate in this little experiment.

"Dear Minnie, you really don't know how much I miss you. I love you so much. I hope you will take me back because if you do, than I will change. You mean the world to me. PS. My friends helped me write this."

I staggered back to the cafeteria dizzily, without Coraline. I'm a snowflake, without my brothers or sisters, alone in the cold world. I landed right in the ocean, where the salt consumed me. Forever and ever, I'll be drifting with the water. I drifted through the hallways, clenching the heart shaped note. I stomped to Clevis with tears filling my eyes. I crumpled it in my clenched fist, and watched as Clevis' face turned grim. As I handed his message, his face went from stern to terrified. It turned pale white, but then he looked determined and desperate, like a bald eagle. At that moment, I knew he'd never stop flying to the fantasy of having me back.

His hands are shaking as he presented a chocolate bar, with almonds in it. He held it out to me, and I took it.

I went back into the hallway steaming. Anger filled inside me as I stomped in circles. Coraline stayed in the cafeteria defending me, as The Wolves complained. I ran away from everyone, and everything. The chocolate is melting in my heated hand.

I locked the bathroom door. After closing it, tears streamed down my face. I slid down the door and slumped on the floor. I choked with anger, reaching the bottom of the abyss, where no light is shown. Here I am, in the restroom, a chocolate bar still laying in my hand. A trash can sat right next to me. As I am about to throw it out, the shiny blue wrapper cried out to me. I cautiously opened it and stared at the chocolate. I slowly bit into it, and Clevis' almond chocolate is delicious. Perhaps almonds aren't all that bad.

February 14th... that is the day to avoid Clevis, and The Wolves. For that one day out of the entire year, I have to ignore these people, no matter what. Even if Center Middle School is in an earthquake, or if the building is on fire, or, if there is an indoor lock-down and we had to fit in the tiny cafeteria, I would still ignore Clevis and The Wolves. It takes courage and persistence to do that, even if he's my worst weakness.

At lunch today, the student council is selling heart shaped balloons, for $1 dollar each. Those small hearts attached to a lollipop stick are the new craze. People are buying those, and presenting it to their crushes, their friends, and a few teachers. The smiles on everybody's faces made me think about giving Clevis a balloon. To thank him for the chocolate, and to make him slightly better. Besides, he must be as devastated as a person living through a break up. While I ignored my urge to ignore him, I asked Coraline for a dollar.

She said no, her face surprised. "For Clevis?"

I nodded, and explained to her why. My table is listening.

"Here's 50 cents," Charlotte said.

"I'm holding 40. What you're doing is good, to make amends!" A girl named Piper said.

"I still need a dime."

Coraline took a dime out of her lunchbox. "Make this worthwhile," she said, handing me the money. I thanked her, knowing she understood my mirror image.

I stood in line to buy a balloon. All of a sudden, I heard squealing behind me. The Wolves are on my list of people to ignore, but it is kind of hard to avoid them.

"Is that for Clevis?" Victoria asked.

I nodded my head, bought the balloon, and ignored all the cheering and chanting. I walked to Clevis' table. Legs a little shaky, knees a bit clammy. I played with my hair, and looked down at my shirt. I gripped the stick, and they looked at me, like I'm a three headed dog. I stared at Clevis like he had four heads. One is beaming, another frowning, one more winking, and the last one in question.

"Clevis, can I see you in the hallway, please?" I asked. His cheeks
went from pink daisy to red rose. I stuffed the tiny balloon in my
pocket. He got up and followed me into the hallway. We stood outside
the door, and the last time we were in this exact spot together, it was at
drama club. Jill used him as a weapon, as a gun, threatening to shoot
me, every time my weakness is in sight.

Here is what I want to say: Clevis, the other day, I was thinking
about the memories we've had. Ice skating at the ice rink, all the laughs
in Science, the facetime calls, lasting the endless night. I miss you, and
those memories. I realized that I do love you. I want you to keep this
heart shaped balloon in admiration of our past and future."

Instead, I said this: "Today is a hard day for myself too. Clevis, I
got you this balloon in honor of our friendship. This is a day of celebration and fondness, but not just about our love, but to respect our relationship," I said. I handed him the symbol of love and he thanked me.
In that moment, Clevis was like a mini cupid, and he struck me with an
arrow. He smiled with sorrow, and walked back into the cafeteria. He
left me standing there, with pure regret. Perhaps Science will be better
today.

"Happy National Heartbreak Day Mrs. Moon!"

Mrs. Moon's room is decorated in a Valentine's spirit. She is the
kind of person to over decorate for the holidays. During Christmas,
she put up a Christmas tree with cheap ornaments. She strung lights
around the room, and placed auburn ribbons on the desks. If this is
a competition between all the classes, then she'd win. The room is
filled with big and shiny plastic hearts. There are balloons of all sizes

everywhere, floating at the ceiling. The desks had the same red ribbons as it did on Christmas. The floors are covered with scarlet glitter and tiny heart shaped sparkles. Instead of a winter wonderland, I could call this a heartbreak wonder world.

My jaw dropped at the sight of it. Mrs. Moon dressed in an all pink and raspberry dress. She had pink face paint, and her frizzy hair had paper hearts in it.

"Wow. You went all out with this!"

Mrs. Moon beamed with pride and got off her ladder. She finished hanging the last of hearts.

"Hey Minnie! You're right, I did over decorate, just the tiniest bit," She admitted.

"It looks... EXTRAORDINARY! I love this room so much," I gasped, noticing the hearts drawn on the whiteboard. Mrs. Moon walked to me, but instead of pride and joy, guilt is written on her face. At that moment, I knew something was wrong. As the student's gathered around the perimeter of the room, something is happening. I'm left standing in the middle, clueless, Mrs. Moon holding a clipboard in her hand.

"Happy Tuesday. I have good news, and horrifying news. As you know, tomorrow is February Vacation, a whole week off from school! That is the good news, and the bad news is that I am placing you into another seating chart. For now, whoever I place you with, this is where you'll be for the rest of the year. I hope these seats will create a convenient learning environment," Mrs. Moon informed. I leaned against the wall, dreading more tension then there is already.

"For your seating chart, it will be the same as the December arrangement" She yelled. From the past two months and twelve days, strain is still in the air. The flashbacks arose...

Imagine yourself in the climax of a movie, with the antagonist rising. I'm the protagonist, in agonising pain, Mrs. Moon controlling it. The smirk on her face made me want to crumple like a piece of paper. I stared at the last three people left. Clevis, the distracting and somewhat demented class clown, and to Coraline, the goth girl with FAILING grades. I gulped, glancing at the last open seats. Well, I lived a decent fourteen years.

"Coraline, Clevis, and let's put Minnie in the middle!" Mrs. Moon exclaimed. While the science class is on Earth, myself, Coraline, and Clevis are on another planet. Now, and forever, I am in the back row, with two monkeys sitting right and left of me. I'm a lone wolf. I'm just the girl in the middle.

But no... I will not let Mrs. Moon control my life the same way she did in December. She KNEW I had a problem with one of my fellow classmates, which made me more angry. With the pressure from The Wolves, and from my own feelings for Clevis, my struggles as a person, it is all because of the December seating chart, and Mrs. Moon knew about it. Besides, in Mrs. Moon's own words, I got to put myself before others in this type of a situation.

"Are you kidding me Mrs. Moon?!" I bellowed, gritting my teeth. As everybody is already in their seats the whole class turned their heads towards me. The Wolves silenced, and Mrs. Moon stepped forward.

"WOW Mrs. Moon. Do you just WANT to see us trying to create DRAMA, so you, as a TEACHER, can sit back and enjoy it?! What the HELL is wrong with you?!" I screamed.

"Minnie..." Mrs. Moon tried.

"No, stop it, you said enough. I HATE this room, and the view from the back of it. You are NOT fit to be a teacher, you should just quit now, and that way, we may be happier without YOU. You disgust me... just, go away now, perhaps jump off a bridge and maybe you won't go to hell..."

Mrs. Moon looked hurt, but I ignored it. "That is no way to--"

Before she completed her sentence, I tore one of her paper hearts. I held up my middle finger at her, making everyone gasp. Coraline made a GTS with her fingers, then made an X, and she looked shocked. Even Coraline wouldn't do something like this. Seeing Clevis look frightened, but for him to be silent... the dictionary defines love as when you have an intense feeling of deep affection, or when you are in a state of fondness and passion. Well, the dictionary can't give the definition of how I feel for him. I missed him, but I'm not sure if I missed him. "WHY IS THIS HAPPENING TO ME?! WHY DID MRS. MOON CREATE ALL OF THIS?!"

Tears filled my eyes, and here I am, standing in the center of attention. I spotted the snowy owl at the window, frowning.

"What is wrong with me Mrs. Moon..." I cried. I see myself leaving the room, hoping to never go back. As I ran farther from the room, I sank deeper into the abyss. I am underwater, trying to breathe a breath of air, but the weight attached to my foot made me sink... deeper and deeper... and deeper... until the door to the school slammed closed.

At this moment, I don't care whether I'm a GTS or not. I don't think leaving is allowed without permission during hours. I cannot believe I just did that. I blew up at Mrs. Moon, in front of the class. I'm not sure what came over me. I felt the urge to scream in her face... I bet most people had that desire... but me, myself and I... I showed it. I spent the afternoon walking a trail, leading to my house. The woods are silent, and as the sun descended, my anger dropped. I became calmer, like the silence around me.

Every so often, I spotted the snowy owl following me, watching closely. She's just an image in my head, just like everything else.

I finally reached my house, ready for the lecture my mother is probably going to give me. She's going to be screaming, yelling, bellowing, and this is the worst National Heartbreak Day ever. As I stepped through the door, there is my mom, on the couch, a glass of wine in her hand.

"Minnie... we need to talk..." She said. I put my Science binder on the table, and joined my mother in the living room.

"Min, Mrs. Moon called me and explained what happened. She sounded very hurt, confused, and most of all, she didn't understand why you would do that kind of a thing," She started. I sat up straight in my chair, scared of what she is going to say next.

"Do you have anything to say about this? The rudeness, the yelling, the middle finger?! I am so disappointed in you, and I thought this went away..." She said.

"What do you mean, gone away?" I asked. She hesitated...

"I know something is wrong with me. What's mistaken with me mom? Why do I interpret the things I do, and why can't I see a problem when there is one? Why do I obsess over certain things? I can see myself being different, and I'm not sure why. It is like my brain is wired differently, and I'm always thinking distinctively different than everyone else."

At that moment, my mother had a concerned look on her face. The same look as when she told me about her divorcing my dad. Just like with my parent's divorce a year ago, I knew that what she would tell me, it will change my life. I sat in silence, waiting for my mother to talk.

"Do you know what autism is?" My mother asked. I heard that word before, but I'm not sure what it conveys. A few people at my school possess it. I wonder why she's bringing it up.

"Why?" My mom hesitated, twirling her hair, covering a shameful face.

"Autism spectrum disorder..." She finally said, "A developmental condition, present from early childhood, characterized by difficulty in communicating and forming relationships with other people and in using language and abstract concepts. This is how the dictionary defines it, and I know you like those definitions."

"I don't understand. What does this have to do with my problems?" I asked, but I knew what was coming.

"Minnie, when you were younger, your father and I noticed a difference with you. For example, your language was delayed, in fact, you didn't speak your first word until you were three years old. I took you to a doctor, and you were clinically diagnosed with PDD-NOS, a form of autism, yes honey, you are on the spectrum. However, you are only mildly affected, and people would only think you're on the quirky side. As you grew older though, your father and I thought you outgrew it, but with Clevis and the seating arrangement, this is somehow bringing all of this back. That is a typical symptom, by obsessing over this and interpreting it wrong."

I sat there, breathing, like my soul has risen from my body. My mind went blank. I wanted the answer to my life for a long time now, because I knew there was something wrong with me. I was not sure whether it was a developmental disability, or just a quality I hold. But now, a new label got put on myself, as being autistic.

"How is this affecting me now?"

"I think you know the answer to that. For some reason, that seating chart, it triggered this to come back. You interpreted yourself completely wrong, thinking you have a new personality because of a seating arrangement. With Clevis, that was wrong from one day, saying he's a Donald Duck in a church choir, to the next, telling people

you love him. All of the people who you think are your friends, like
The Wolves Pack, aren't. They're making fun of you and Clevis, and
you didn't register it. Sometimes, you don't realize when you can
get yourself into some serious drama like this, and Minnie, it isn't
your fault either. That is also why you blew up at Mrs. Moon. During
elementary school, you lost many friendships without realizing it,
you had an IEP, an Individual Education Plan, and yet, you thought
of yourself as being normal. I'm sorry your Dad and I didn't tell you
earlier, but we didn't want you to put a label on yourself. Minnie, did
you know Albert Einstein was and Bill Gates is autistic? A delightful
part of being on the mild side of the spectrum is how uncommon you
are. You're unique, you are an extraordinary artist, and you're like a
snowy owl even. You may have autism, but being autistic doesn't define
you," my mother ended.

I have a lot in common with the moon. Dark clouds covered the
only light filling the night sky. I leaned up against a tree. Bark scratched
my back and tall grass hugged my legs. Extensive breaths I took, very
deep gulps of air. My brain fell to the core of regret. My heart sank
lower than the depths of hell. I sank to the bottom of the abyss. The
only thing I hold now is... the truth.

The truth on how The Wolves are talking behind my back, and the
truth of my feelings for Clevis. The truth of the pressure around me,
and the truth of being in the middle of a seating chart... I frowned at the
sights of my memories from today. National Heartbreak Day... it happens every year.

After I left the school, I wrote a message to myself on the same
heart shaped sticky notes Clevis gave me. That the dictionary defines

love as when you have an intense feeling of deep affection, or when you are in a state of fondness and passion. Well, the dictionary can't give the definition of how I feel towards him.

I pulled out the heart shaped letter from my pocket. In the sky above me, I spotted an orange blur. A tangerine blur turning into a feather. An owl landed on my shoulder and I felt a warm sensation right from my shoulders to my toes. I huffed in deeply once again, bottling up tears.

I wanted to soothe the warmth of the sun, the life of Earth, the grand size of Jupiter. I longed to wear the rings of Saturn, and to swim in the waves of Neptune. I desire to blush the color of Mars, but to felt the frigid temperature in Uranus. I wished to stand at the height of Venus, and craved to be like the roman god of Mercury. I desire to hold the Milky Way galaxy in my clammy palms. I know for a fact that I wanted love. To be idolized, to let me love myself, to love my life the way it is, and love myself for who I am. It is just not possible right now.

It may never be. That is the truth.

With the simple thought of that, I stared at the owl in her bright golden eyes. Patterns and lines filled her gleaming pupils. Her feathery eyebrows marginally covering the moonlight reflecting her eyes. In her eyes, I didn't just see an eye, I gazed into my reflection.

"Why me, myself, and I..."

Another tear dropped on the soft soil. The owl hooted, and it echoed throughout the forest. Her beak didn't move, but so many words repeated in my head over and over again. She whisked away into the night sky, bringing the moon out of the clouds. That owl stands out from the crowd, like myself. Moonlight shimmered on me, like a rainfall of peaceful bliss.

Indeed, I do hold the truth.

I texted Clevis the truth. We got back together, and on the last few seconds of Valentines Day.

Chapter 7

My blades hit the ice like the sweet sound of a bat hitting a base-ball. Stride by stride I strided, the scent of natural ice made my eyes bulge out. I roved through the moist, crispy, ice, frigid, air. My hair whipped with the sharp turns I produced. Ice skating is like the saying, "practice makes perfect," but personally, I don't believe that. Nothing is ideal, while no person is suitable when it comes to this skill. Yet, we all retain coming back, we maintain making mistakes, but we keep on learning.

This is the last day of February vacation, and tomorrow, the mis-take I made will backfire on me the second I walk into Mrs. Moon's science classroom. Today, there are bigger things to worry about. Ever since our field trip to the ice skating rink in December, I've been going ice skating several times. A few with my friends, a few with my father, and once with Coraline even. Clevis has been begging me to go with him. For all of this week, he's been constantly texting me, and from the results of that, we made plans to go ice skating. Today will be a pretty daunting feat.

When I broke up with Clevis in January, I fell into an endless abyss, or so I thought. Now, I climbed out, like climbing a vertical mountain. I reached the top of Mount Everest and I could see everything going on in the world. People are microscopic, and clouds blurred them. I breathed the diligent air, and touched the moon with my palm. The moon gleamed at me, and brightened the world, just like how I lightened after Clevis and I got back together. Clevis and I... we are back.

"You two are back?" My dad asked, taking a right turn.

"Yes, and you've asked that almost a million times now! Yes, we are back!"

After I told my dad the exciting news, he acted like I dropped a bomb on him. I remember that same night, there he was, eating bucket loads of ice cream.

"Do you love him Min? Because you hesitated the last time I asked."

"Dad, we just got back together."

"Why?" He asked. There are some questions in this world, that are just too personal to answer.

"Why not?" I answered.

"There are loads of reasons why you shouldn't be with him."

I groaned and was glad when we pulled into Clevis' driveway. Our reunion is going to be at his front door, in front of his parents, and my dad is planning to stay in the car. The temptation to bolt inside his house is hard to resist. The tension is killing me as I stepped out of the car, and this is far worse than standing around the perimeter, dreading a new seating chart.

His house is the same from when I last came here. He still had sleds out, with snow on them. I remembered the time we went sledding, and now I'm laughing about it. I'm just glad winter's almost over, so we won't have to that again, ever again. Once again, his front door is calling my name.

The moment has arrived for me to be one lucky bride. Imagining myself in a wedding dress, I knocked on the front door. Well, if Mr. Cleveland opened the door to see me as a bride, his reaction will be like my dads when I told him about Clevis. Truth is, I expected Mr. Cleveland to be enraged, considering how I embarrassed Clevis to death a month ago. I would expect them to give me a lecture, then I'll turn this into a debate, than I'll end up lecturing him on the importance of seating charts and their consequences. For everything that happened in the past three months I'm blaming Mrs. Moon. Mr. Cleveland opened the door, and my eyes bulged out at his friendly face.

"Hey Minnie! It is nice to see you again!" He greeted warmly.

"Hello Mr. Cleveland, I hope your day is going well. Thank you for letting my father and I take Clevis to the ice skating rink for extracurricular activity," I said. All of a sudden, I heard a repeated sound of hops down the stairway. Clevis came around the corner, gleaming like a groom seeing his wife in a wedding dress. We stood together, like the classic plastic bride and groom on a wedding cake. Our cake had multiple layers, some good, some bad, but at the top we are together. Right now, I'm eating the most delicious slice. The slice of life.

"CLEVIS!!!!"

I clapped my hands, excited to see his smiling face.

"Hey Minnie!!! It is so so so great to see you!!!" Clevis brightened, happy to see my smiling face.

On the way to the ice rink, we passed Center Middle School. Twenty four hours from now, Clevis and I will be sitting in the back row, with a deadly secret. Earlier this week, Clevis and I texted how we're going to keep The Wolves away from us.

"Are we going to try to stand up to them?!" he asked.

"I have no idea. They'll be happy to hear about this. I have not told anybody yet, but if I do, I want to see their reaction in person," I responded. He sent a heart emoji.

"I agree. Still, I don't want our relationship to be about the reactions of other people, or anything having to do with other people. I don't want The Wolves absorbed in this. It seems like they're involved with EVERYTHING!!" He said, replying with another heart emoji.

"I am so sick of them, and I wish they knew what I had so they can stop bothering us. Nevertheless, if they knew, they are mean enough to treat me the same," I said, sending a crying emoji.

He sent several colored heart emojis.

I texted again. "Perhaps we can keep this a secret, so nobody at our school will know. We can work on avoiding drama, and if The Wolves bug us... like what happened the day before Valentine's Day, then the both of us can stand up to them. We can tell them to stop."

He sent a heart emoji.

"I couldn't agree with this idea more! Only our parents will know."

I sent a smiling emoji.

He sent a heart emoji.

With this secret on our minds, it will be hard to keep it. We both crossed our hearts and hoped to die, stick a needle in our eye. Not only that, but we're taking this secret to the grave.

"Minnie, I'm going to be a little rough, and I may stay on the side. I haven't skated since the field trip," Clevis uttered.

"We can manage."

This time should be easier, considering the progress he made last time. This brings me back to the time Clevis was about to go on the ice for the first time. "Clevis, remember when you first stepped on the ice? You wouldn't let go of the side. But soon... you did!" I said.

"But then I fell over again, and I sprained my ankle, and it was because of you," He said.

"Then again, you did let go of the side in the first place. Besides, the thing about ice skating is that anybody can be good at it, but we just need to practice. By falling over, we can only improve by that. So in that case, good job!" I said, winning the debate.

I held his hand and leaned in closer. "I won't let go this time."

As we stepped on the ice, he slanted on me. He is dependent of me, like I'm holding onto his life. I clasped his life in my own hands, but soon, I started to let go of him. As he unattached himself, he immediately let go. He strided once.

He fell over.

"Listen Clevis, honey, you have to let go of the wall or else, sweetie, you will never make progress, sweetheart," I calmly told him. Even though I acted calm and collected, my teeth are gritting, and making a silent squeaky chalkboard sound. I wanted to rip my blade off my skate, storm to Clevis, and convince him to let go of the wall during the field trip.

And once again, I want to rip my blade off, tell Clevis to stop crying, and to stand up from the floor. Clevis is still on the ground, moaning and groaning. "I can't do this," He cried, slightly shaking. Giving up is never an option, because when you give up on something, it doesn't benefit you in any way. The only time you should truly give up is when the whole world is against each other, and when we are all unhappy, like in the two world wars. When the world is suffering with pain, and when there is nothing we can do. That will be when we give up, but that won't happen for a while, certainly not today, and definitely not while Clevis and I are trying to ice skate.

"You'll never make progress if you're more glued to the side than a root is to a tree. Clevis, I'm sorry for not helping you up on the field trip. I shouldn't of given up. I am here now, and I always will be."

I spoke my mind, and the truth. All of a sudden, I caught sight of something. I gripped on Clevis' hand, and dragged him as fast as possible. I found somewhere to hide, and I shoved Clevis and myself into that hiding place.

"Minnie, what are you doing?!" He asked. "Be quiet, don't let yourself be seen, and look at the entrance."

The Wolves are here. Is this merely a coincidence?

"Did you tell The Wolves about us?!" He shook his head, and asked me the same question. "No, of course not."

Why are they here... I wondered to myself. There's Victoria, dressed in a puffy white dress, white figure skates, and white earmuffs. Following her is Aneska, wearing black, then Jill, wearing the grey scale. Clevis and I have to somehow escape, but it is disappointing because I won't be able to teach him. It seems as though The Wolves are always getting in the way of our happiness. Like Clevis texted me earlier this week, they have to be involved with EVERYTHING.

"Minnie, maybe we can just go out there and say we're friends," Clevis suggested. "We can't risk that," I said back. When it comes to The Wolves, we can't take chances with anything, or it can ruin our lives for a lifetime.

They left after an hour. Clevis and I came out of our hiding spot, legs cramped, feet asleep, and hands clenched. We had five minutes until my dad is going to pick us up. "Clevis, I am so sorry about this," I groaned.

For the first time in forever, he let go of the side, himself, without my help. Clevis waved his arms and juggled his skates so they could start moving. With each small stride he took, he traveled a small amount of distance. I followed behind him, and I balanced on my two blades, and I hoped for the best. I was ready to catch him if he ever fell. I have full trust in him, even if he is skating on the behalf of my treacherous teaching life. Even though Victoria may have caught sight of us, nothing can get in the way of how proud I am.

"You are flying at the speed of light!" I sang. I kissed him on the forehead.

When I walked through the doors to the science room, students are around the perimeter of the room. Mrs. Moon held a clipboard, and stood right in the center. She glanced at me, and I could still see the pain in her dark brown eyes. Her black frizzy hair covered the shameful face, and this is the thing I dreaded for most of February vacation. I strolled behind her, hoping to never look at her face again.

"Welcome back everybody. As we are entering into March, we'll be looking deeper into our galaxy and beyond that. In about a month, you and your group are going to plan an oral presentation to present for an exam grade. After the... incident... that happened last week, I have a new seating chart. It is--"

"MRS. MOON!!! NOW MINNIE AND I CAN BE IN LOVE AGAIN. THANK YOU LADIES AND GENTLEMAN, AND TO THIS BEAUTIFUL GIRL!!!" He roared, interrupting the talking teacher. Well, he broke the secret, and I lived a decent fourteen years. Coraline can plan my funeral. On my gravestone, it will say, "R.I.P. Minnie Ann Stickley-Adotte. Died of a seating chart". In Mrs. Moon's science class-room, it is silent, more quiet than the silence has ever been.

"Impossible," Mrs. Moon breathed.

Chapter 8

This started with a seating chart. This, a simple seating chart which turned into the new Netflix show most people are obsessing over. In those, there is a surprise in every corner, rumors roaming the streets, and people would create marathons to binge watch these kinds of shows. The season finale ended the second after Clevis announced our engagement. Oh yes, for this episode, it might as well break a record for most viewers in the shortest period of time. The first person to piece the puzzle together was Mrs. Moon, who gasped, "Impossible." If I had to give a definition of 'impossible', I would describe this moment, and the moments to come. I looked at the ceiling to avoid her, along with everyone else's expression. That same day, two catastrophes happened. A tragic seating chart, and the great announcement, loud enough for the whole school to hear.

The timing was right as the bell rang. I remember melodramatically bolting out of the room, grasping my backpack, and dashing out of the building. Clevis was the match to start the fire, and now, I see big and beautiful scorching flames. Their burning over our secret, and dissolving it as though the secret was written on a piece of paper.

I didn't see Clevis come out until my bus left the parking lot. A mob of girls hovered over him, a pack of Wolves. I took one glance at him, and he was surrounded. He is calm and collected though, like he meant to reveal our secret.

"Why the great announcement Clev?" I texted.

"Well... I just, blurted it.... Besides, I don't think either one of us could keep this secret for that long."

I didn't blame him. That secret has been a weight on my shoulders since the second we got together, and I wanted to tell The Wolves so many times. During vacation, they wouldn't stop bothering me. I got constant text messages and emails from Jill. She seemed like the most eager wolf to get us back, and this brought me to the memory of the geography bee. I remember Clevis walking out with her, holding hands and laughing.

"Do you still like Jill?"

"I love you. Do we have drama club next Friday?" He replied. I sent a smiling emoji to him, and I got a little excited. Drama club is starting to be more frequent. One of the things I adore in drama club is when scenes are beginning to piece together like a puzzle. When the leads start singing well and expanding their voices when saying lines. When dancers in the dance numbers are starting to bring together their routine. Where the backstage crew starts ruling the place. I would say that we are on our way to becoming professionals.

You may expect a gigantic theater with ruby red curtains, or a golden stage floor where an actor or actress can shine like a Hollywood star. The lights made the stage look like Rockefeller Center during the Christmas season. Rows of cushioned seats with those fancy numbers on each of them. An experienced director who creates Broadway plays and musicals. Props that take days, or weeks, to paint by hand. The Lion King's masks, Hamilton's history concepts, and the wicked witches, who make the musical, well, Wicked. Even Dear Evan Hansen and its beautiful harmonies. And Aladdin, who makes Broadway into a whole new world. What you might expect in a drama club.... well, that's not us.

As the flashback came back to me, I realized that this may be as lovely as Broadway is. Now that we are a month from the opening night of the musical, we are having drama club once a week, every Friday, and soon to be twice a week. The more frequent drama club is, the more drama there will be.

The second I walked into the cafeteria, I felt like Santa Clause. A million kids sending me letters and demanding gifts. Them hovering over me, looking up at my wisdom, asking sacred questions about my relationship. One by one, standing in line to either ask a question about insight on my personal life, or, to request something having to do with my private life. To them, Clevis and I are their Christmas miracle.

"Hey folks!" Mrs. Short babbled, clapping her hands. Today we are going to go through the bigger scenes and practice the dance numbers. And let me remind you, if you aren't in any of those, than please sit quietly and do some schoolwork. You may also socialize with your friends. Just, make sure you're quiet. Let's do the First Time in Forever dance number first! Before I let you go, I know that all of you have grown in your parts. I just wanted to say that everyone has a part in this. Even if you got one as small as, a tree, then you want to be the best darn tree there is!" Mrs. Short finished. The kids hanging on me let go and joined the dance.

Mr. Clause and I journeyed to the north pole to avoid The Wolves. In the back of the cafeteria, we sat down in our imaginary thrones. Before having the chance to relax, Jill and Aneska sit down next to us. Look! The kids on the naughty list!

"Minnie, Clevis, we, The Wolves, decided to do a couples counseling for you two lovebirds," Jill declared. Another way to say couples counseling is relationship therapy, and that is when you open up about your issues, and try to solve them with your partner. Insanity has taken over The Wolves... they want to do this for us. Obviously, they're stirring up trouble.

"We don't require couples counseling. Clevis and I are in a perfectly fine relationship right now."

While they think they're turning over a new leaf, here's my leaf,
losing its color and beauty. My season is revolving to winter, where
trees and plants die. There are no need for new leaves, or new 'couples
counseling'.

"You dumped Clevis because of your issues with him... you broke
up with him in front of the entire school! There were tears, fights, overthinking... You never got a chance to talk to him about it. We don't want
this to happen again, because you two are the couple of the year, voted
by us. Aneska, Coraline, and I will be controlling it, even though Victoria thought of the idea. Whenever we are off stage, we will be counseling," Jill asserted softly.

"We'll be doing several activities and keeping track of the actions
you do. For example, towards the end of our sessions, we'll each be
writing a list of complaints about one another. Along with that, we will
be observing you, taking notes, recording what you say, and we will
start planning for your bright future," Aneska explained. I think they
rehearsed this conversation.

"Coraline, why are you here? Don't you hate me?" Clevis asked.
Coraline stood behind me, holding a ruler in her hand in place of a baton.

"I just want to see where this goes. It is hysterical!" Coraline said,
laughing. She's like a new person, her cooperating with The Wolves.
She hates them, and they despise her, but they all have one thing in
common; to keep MY relationship with Clevis alive.

In Science last year, the most boring unit was the ecosystems and
living factors one. I used to be bored out of my mind, but I do remember one thing, and only one thing about it. A live thing is an alive thing

if it can move, grow, reproduce, and If it has cells. This counseling is similar to that because The Wolves want to heal this living thing, so Clevis and I can move, grow, but not to reproduce.

"SNOWFLAKES, SNOWFLAKES, I NEED MY SNOW-FLAKES", Mrs. Short yelled, signaling the end of our first 'couples counseling'. Aneska handed me an appointment reminder slip, and apparently, it needs a parent signature.

Back when I was younger, I could've had a career in making puzzles, or inventing the jigsaw puzzle, or, I could called myself The Puzzle Queen. Puzzles come naturally to me, as my dad had said. On a rainy day when I was three, I scrambled three 100 piece puzzles so they were mixed. My dad runs a few errands and an hour later, he comes back to find all three together. He even called the doctor to see if I'm some sort of a genius, but then that day, apparently, I got diagnosed with something far worse. Ever since then, I figured out all sorts of mysteries, math equations, rubix cubes, and the lines missing in my drawings.

When something pieces together, it feels like the most extraordinary thing in the world. You could finally understand the situation, and when that magical moment arrives, you are relieved, like you found the answer to another question in life. This can relate to when a drama club performance pieces together. As Mrs. Short stated at the beginning of the year, we'll be working on the separate scenes until they magically combine. A masterpiece after months of work, months of hard labor, months of practice, but months for one goal. The one drama club meeting when everything connects, and creates the full musical. That would be a satisfaction to anybody, to know that we created something remarkable.

"Hi folks! If you know how to read a calendar, then you know today is March 17th, which means we have two weeks until our opening night, which is on the 30th. Then, a second and third showing, going into April. Now that we know what we're doing and how much time we have left, these are the weeks where you really have to FOCUS the most. I want this whole club to pay attention, and I am aware of the drama going around in this drama club, so let's not create drama, however, let's master drama!" Mrs. Short informed, glaring at us.

She continued talking. "Today will be the day we finally do a full run through! As I said at the beginning of the year, we will eventually have that one rehearsal where the scenes come together. So let's get whipped into shape! The opening scene is where we're starting, obviously. I will give you five minutes to prepare. And remember, NO SCRIPTS," Mrs. Short shouted. She jumped down from the chair she is standing on, and started tweaking the DVD player. Like how she was tweaking that, I am jerking the grueling puzzle of The Wolves and drama. It has been harder than a 5,000 piece jigsaw puzzle.

"Minnie and Clevis, look over there," Coraline whispered. Here is where the drama club officially starts. The directors are Victoria, Aneska, and Jill, and their play is named "disaster". Their stage is in the back of the room, and they are waving at the lead roles, Clevis and I. I regretted auditioning for this, but as I said once before, the rule of thumb is to listen to The Wolves.

"Hello lovebirds!" Victoria chirped. Just a few weeks ago, she was the most pressuring and nasty person, but now she's acting the opposite of herself. And now, she's calling us birds and offering us couples counseling. Her mood swings and opinions are like a roller coaster because Clevis and I are both throwing up. I clenched Clevis' fist and went to the table in the back of the room.

"Clevis and I are functioning on our own right now, so I don't understand why you're concerned about our relationship. It is like you care about my life more than your own. We don't want couples counseling!"

"Minnie Ann Stickley-Adotte, you NEED this," She insisted.

"NO, not really," I told her in a gruff voice. "Like I said before, we are FINE."

"Whether you like it or not, you are doing this!" Victoria snapped. She gave me a dirty smirk and grasped my arm. Her long and pointy nails dug into my skin when I tried to resist sitting down, but she shoved me down.

"Sit down sweetie. My colleagues and I will take care of this."

Clevis immediately sat down next to me. He doesn't want to be pushed around like a slave... he just followed the rules, like the rule of thumb says.

"Minnie and Clevis, I would like to introduce the activity we will be performing today. Before we talk to the crease of your inner problems, we will be doing a social experiment that will give you two relationship confidence. We will be walking around the room and asking people of their opinions of this relationship. Then, you two will take notes on what they say. If the comment is negative, you will learn that comments can't come in the way of your love. If it is positive, then this is a good sign," Jill directed.

"I will give you paper and my own signature sparkly pencils," Aneska chimed in. She handed both of us a glittering pencil with pink feathers, a purple eraser, and her name is engraved into it. This pencil reminds me of a typical Wolf, and I used this to write a recipe for disaster. I clasped it and followed Jill to our first suspect, like the follower I am.

She led us to a junior Wolf, Penelope. Penelope is holding a box of tissues and blowing her nose. A few months ago, Penelope qualified to be an official Wolf, so I remember Jill mentoring her. Penelope is very prone to getting sick. Her face is always red and she's always carrying around pills and medications. She would not stop coughing during The Wolves meetings, and her Wolf career ended when she sneezed on Jill, and she didn't mean too! They got disgusted by her sickness and stopped talking to her, at least until right now.

"Hi Penelope!" Jill greeted, like nothing ever happened.

She sneered and gave Jill a glare.

"Anyway... we need your opinion on Clevis' and Minnie's relationship," Jill said. Penelope curled her lip once again, than she coughed, then she glared again.

"I cannot believe you dragged me into this stupid relationship thing with poor Minnie, and kudos to Clevis also. What do I think of their relationship you ask? I think the only reason they got back together is from the pressure from you popular gals," Penelope shared. She stormed away and went to blow her nose again. Her face is redder than a sick person vomiting all harsh words for The Wolves to clean up. I want to be like that. It must be nice to be Penelope.

"Alright, Minnie, Clevis, write that down," Aneska murmured. We are both startled, but we wrote down, *don't meddle with things.*

Jill shrugged it off, and we moved to the next victim. I feel bad for whoever's next on their long list. And of course, my former crush is on the list. The international Spanish star who'd gain a career from playing Kristof in this musical. During Rogelio's audition, I almost cried after watching him sing because it was just so beautiful. Poor, innocent, Rogelio, who is actually focusing... it is a shame how Aneska has to bother him, on stage, right now. I stand there, viewing Aneska beg Rogelio for an opinion. As I watched them, Clevis and Jill stood next to each other, them both staring at me.

Aneska came back, vigorously writing. This is the one and only,

Rogelio's view on a relationship with plutonium involved. I wondered numerous times whether he has feelings for me, or how jealous he is of Clevis and I. I proceeded with caution as I took the paper from Aneska... that has a million expressions fitted into three sentences. "I think Minnie and Clevis are a lovely couple. But if Minnie did this to make me jealous, then it didn't work. They should only stay together if they truly love each other." I wrote, *Never follow your heart if you want to make others fell nasty.*

"Alright Minnie, Clevis, guess who's next on our list?"

I'm wondering who's going to be embarrassed next. This is getting out of hand, but being me, there is nothing I can do to stop it. I grudged on Aneskas pink sparkly pencil, like I'm holding on a tightrope for my life, over the Niagara Falls. Whoever this next person is, I hope I'm strong enough to not fall off.

We went to Coraline next, who is pretending to smoke a cigarette in the corner. I could tell she's trying to hold in laughter, but it only came out as a snicker.

"You want MY opinion? I think this is hysterical, this whole thing. However, beyond the couples therapy, I don't believe that Minnie is following her heart. Truth is, I think she should find a relationship with herself before she can allow herself to love another geek."

Coraline waved us off, and winked at me before we traveled to the next person. I wrote down, *To have a relationship with someone else, you should be in a relationship with yourself first.*

"Okay, now let's have a GOOD opinion. Let's go to Victoria!" She squealed. Her and Aneska ran to the stage, and did some sort of a handshake with Victoria. They asked for her belief, and she screamed to Clevis and I "YOU ARE THE COUPLE OF THE CENTURY." I wrote down, *Victoria is crazy.*

Besides that, most people's opinions were negative to Clevis and I being together. Whenever we did a pessimistic review, Jill would take us to another Wolf. On my paper, I had a variety of sentences, and with each sentence written, my smile became lower until it became a frown.

"Mrs. Short!" Jill screeched.

"No way... that is a TEACHER."

But I'm too late, Jill is already running to her. Several Wolves followed us this time, snickering behind us and covering their mouths. Being the kind of teacher Mrs. Short is, I have no idea what her reaction will be. In fact, you can never know when teachers are talking about their students in the sacred teacher's lounge. They could say anything, spread around gossip, and you never know what they said about Clevis and I.

The next thing I know, here I am, standing next to Mrs. Short, with Jill asking her opinion. Mrs. Short glanced to Clevis and I.

"Minnie and Clevis got back together? I knew that... I saw it in People Magazine!" She answered. Clevis smiled like he's a model on the front of People Magazine, then he started jumping up and down, which a celebrity wouldn't do on the cover of People Magazine.

"WOW! Really Mrs. Short?!"

I slapped my forehead.

"Honey, yes I did!"

"Where were you?" He asked.

"I was at the salon... Clevis... do you actually believe me?" She inquired.

"Well... well... well... maybe..."

He blushed, and covered his face from the shrieks of The Wolves. They broke out laughing, and with this activity, they got to their goal of laughing their heads off.

What did I write on my page? *Our relationship isn't famous yet, but the teachers are making fun of it. Be careful in this generation.*

Jill ran after Clevis and comforted him before I could. That scene ended and we once again, traveled to the back of the room. Aneska graded my paper, marking corrections with her red pen. I kept my eye on the musical coming together. Everyone's singing is almost perfect, and the transitions are a little rocky. I heard the stage crew giving orders, knowing what to do, but overall, this is coming together, like a puzzle.

Piecing together a puzzle can be tricky in some cases, because it can be a simpler puzzle where it is the drama club coming together, or it can be the puzzle of life, and figuring out everybody's opinions on things. With those pieces of the puzzle, they may be missing, or hard to put together. By the time Jill and Aneska finished, I had fifteen beliefs written down on paper. These judgments are like writing a book, because the positives are like complimenting your story line, but negatives are feedback to improve your story. Still, like I said, we got almost all positives, but we also got missing puzzle pieces.

"Hi folks, you will never believe it but we have exactly one week before opening night!!" Mrs. Short announced. "If you have the ability to read a calendar, than you will know that today is March 24th. I will need your full attention because this last week can be the most stressful and nerve racking. At our last meeting, we had a little trouble staying on track, which is not good. Today, we will go through every scene, in ordinal numbers, so EVERYBODY, positions! NOW!" Mrs. Short ordered. She's a ship captain and we're all pirates going under her command. We all hopped on stage and waited for the next order. The Wolves are searching for their treasure, for Clevis and I. Speaking of couples counseling, I 'forgot' the second appointment card. Sometimes,

I feel like there are always cameras around me when I'm in couples counseling.

I whispered to Coraline, who stood next to me. "Do we have therapy today? Because since we only have a week until the musical..."

"I have no idea. But after the last time, when you were asking people for their opinions, I thought The Wolves were taking this too far. I know what they want, but at the same time, it is as confusing as hell," Coraline mentioned. I asked Clevis what he thought.

"I think I'm always being pressured by them, and I'm getting sick of being treated like an object. Honestly, Jill is the only nice person in the group," He mumbled.

"I desire to punch Victoria in the face, because she doesn't know one thing about the way I am," I sighed. I wish Victoria knew how I'm functioned so she'd stop pressuring Clevis and I. She should leave us alone so we can deal with our own problems.

"Well Minnie, there is one word out there, by the name of "ignore." You can't let them get to your head, because you're your own person. And don't tell Victoria about the thing I think you're thinking about. That'll be worse than what the seating chart created," Coraline concluded. I stood in between Clevis and Coraline, right below the stage where the stars shine. I want to climb there, and give The Wolves a piece of my mind.

"CLEVIS! MINNIE! I know exactly what activity we are doing today,' Aneska interposed, sneaking up behind us. She looked at her diamond watch. "In fact, let's do it right now."

Aneska brought Clevis and I to the table in the back of the cafeteria, like we are prisoners, holding grudge against top notch police men. Coraline and Jill followed, like the witnesses they seem to be. Coraline walked around us, carrying a ruler in place of a baton, hiding a smirk.

"I'm sorry, but I forgot my appointment ca-."

"That doesn't matter, but your love DOES matter," Jill interrupted, confidently. These Wolves just adore interrupting us kids on a lower class level.

"Minnie, Clevis, Clevis, Minnie, after a successful meeting last week, we are going to step up the stairs, if you know what I mean. Today, we are asking the basic questions about your relationship. Along with that, Aneska and I will be recording what you say, and we'll start planning your future," Jill noted. I'm wondering how far into the future she's talking about.

"First, why did you two lovebirds get back together?" she asked. That's a simple question with a complicated answer. I can't explain to them the reasons why, even though it is explainable, but if it is barely explainable to me, than it will be unexplainable to them. Nevertheless, they weren't the ones who were comparing themselves to the moon.

"I missed him."

Clevis eyed me, he found the hesitation in my answer.

"Why did you break up with--?"

"Why did you get together with him in the first place?" Jill piled on.

"What do you see in Clevis?" Victoria asked, coming upon us.

"Do you love each other?!" They all asked, at the same time.

"If you want all the answers in the world, than ask Mrs. Moon about her December seating chart," I replied. I got up, and left, and I wanted to run away. I would sprint all over the country, like Forrest Gump did, and dart away from reality for a while. I'll zoom across, through, and to the other side of the world. As far away from The Wolves as possible.

"WAIT! MINNIE! COME BACK HERE! We have to start planning for the future! We have to finish the lesson!! Final question. "How long do you think you will be together?" They asked. Clevis stared at me with a spark in his eyes.

"A lifetime..." he answered, somewhat staring at Jill, but I didn't think anything of it.

"Seriously Clevis? A lifetime is until the day we're dead. Imagine this; In eighty years, us sitting out on a creaky wooden porch, our kids loathing in our country field trying to take care of the pigs and cows, while you are tipping yourself over to pay taxes on time. We would have nobody living around us, and I'll just live with a mental disease, wasting away my life! In the 3000's, we would be alive on a farm, and we would also die on a farm."

For my time with Clevis, I'll give it a month.

One of my personality traits is the skill of complaining, and the ability to feel decent after protesting about something. Ever since I was young, I had a friend by the name of Piper. Piper and I would enjoy the art of whining all the time. We were masters at our favorite hobby, grumbling about being cold outside at recess, or how the school rules work. We'd complain about political issues, and our siblings and friends, and even a variety of seating charts over the years. In fact, I'd write essays on grousing about something. Papers long enough to reach the hot burning sun. My essays would be on fire, so I considered joining a debate club once. I'm good at getting into debates with The Wolves, especially in couples counseling.

"If you can read a calendar, then you will know that today is March 29th, and that tomorrow is our first showing. We will be doing a full run through I hope you brought your costumes because this is the dress rehearsal. As you can see, we have our sound equipment, our sets and props, and well, everything we need. This is the real deal kids, at least for the dress rehearsal!" Mrs. Short cheered.

Chairs are lined up in the hallway, one for every actor and actress. I put my backpack on the of the chairs, but I almost tripped over one of the props. This place is a mess, but it is a beautiful mess. Paper snowflakes are all over the floor, wigs, dresses, and this place is a Frozen wonderland. This place is more decorated for winter than Mrs. Moon's room was for Valentine's Day. Speaking of love...

"Well, today will be the last couples counseling session, so that is something to celebrate! Because after, we'll all be focused on the show, then after drama club ends, there will be no more counseling! Truth is, the only reason why I supported these sessions is because this is downright hysterical. As much as I would love to punch Victoria in the face, this is HILARIOUS," She said, breaking down laughing.

I chuckled to myself. The concept in this may be funny to a person who isn't being pressured, but not in my point of view. Aneska and Jill sat in the chairs next to us. Aneska clenched a clipboard with her face implanted on it, and Jill held a stack of paper with The Wolves signature pink sparkly pencils.

"Hello Clevis and Minnie, we have an activity planned, specified by our leader, Victoria. This is the session where we'll arrive at the core of your problems with each other, than after, we can try to resolve them. Aneska and I will give you both a piece of paper and you will write a list of complaints about one another. The categories you can choose from is appearance, personality, actions, movements, or anything for that matter. You two will split up for now. Clevis and I will stay here. Minnie, Aneska, and Coraline, go to the other side of the hallway. You will have ten minutes to write as many complaints as possible. Be gone," Jill commanded.

If I was in elementary school again, I would've loved to complain about Clevis. But if I was younger, I wouldn't figure out how much it would hurt him. My list will be as deep as The Pacific Ocean goes, because it could drown both Clevis and I. There we are, sinking to the bottom, one mile for every sentence we write. Chains attached to our feet, and when I got my paper and pencil, I started on his appearance section. I know I shouldn't be doing this, but I kept on writing and feeling bad with every word written down. I'm in a place where it is pitch black, like it is once again, an abyss fallen into.

I looked over at Clevis, and his pencil isn't making marks. Him and Jill are bickering with each other, as he refused to write any complaints about me. All of a sudden, he blushed at her, and her face reddened back. Aneska, Coraline, and I stared at them, like we're all statues. They're like statues staring into one another, my eyes are stuck on Clevis, then there are the statues of Aneska and Coraline, glaring at Jill. Clevis kept the gaze the longest.

They left, and went to the Science hallway. I found myself breathing deeply, almost out of breath, like I am sinking in everlasting water.

"C'mon Min, let's follow him," Coraline said. Coraline and I stood up, and I was shaking again. "Aneska, are... are... are you coming?"

"Minnie, for once, I don't think it's right for me to be immersed in this," Aneska accepted. Common sense finally got knocked into her brain. Coraline and I crawled until we caught a glimpse of them, in the Science hallway. We leaned in a bit close to eavesdrop, and what he said broke me.

"Jill, I like you. I'm not sure about Minnie. She's just, not as exemplary as you," Clevis told her. Coraline whispered a swear to me. He reached out his hand and pressed it with hers.

She blushed, but backed away. "Clevis, you have to stay loyal to Minnie, because she's a kind-hearted person, even though my group may not say it all the time," She said.

I peered at my list of complaints, with one hundred sentences, one hundred bullets, one hundred heartbreakers, one hundred objections. I wrote one more complaint, how he has feelings for Jillian James. Now I know why he agreed to couples counseling, and insisted on staying with her several times, and I now understand his actions towards her. Yet, being me, I would've never understood what's been going on.

"Clevis..."

The echo traveled through the hallway, and reached him in a heartbeat. I walked to him, like I'm walking into my own abyss. An abyss full of darkness, of hatred, of reject and neglect, an abyss where I, myself, where I belong. I opened my list, and Clevis read every complaint, and with every complaint his eyes gazed over, a tear dropped from his tinted hazel eyes.

"Goodbye Minnie," He said.

Clevis walked away, crumpling my list, and my heart in his bare hands.

I sank deeper...

And deeper...

And deeper...

Until the owl inside of me drowned.

Chapter 9

Frozen, Night One

All he said was goodbye, and farewell was all he said. There is no word more understandable than adios. Bye, means the parting of two people, or the separation of them, or the end to something. Not only did I say see you later to Clevis, but I also said cheerio to myself. I remember it like it was yesterday, me crawling through the hallway with Coraline. I saw the worst sight any girlfriend could see. My heart breaking, and after Clevis walked away, I collapsed. There was Jill and Coraline asking if I was okay, but I didn't say anything, because there was nothing more to be said. I wasn't sure if he was signaling a break up, or not, or a fight, or a separation, or a vacation, but either way, I'm not sure how long he had feelings for Jill. It could've been for the longest time, but being the person I am, I probably wouldn't have figured it out.

Couples counseling got decimated like a bomb going off on Valentine's Day. An explosion happened, like when your life explodes into tiny little slices. You don't know which pieces are missing, or where to go to find them, because you don't know where you belong, and you don't know what to do next.

When I trudged back into the drama club hallway, Victoria comforted me. I spotted other people staring, who were watching us. Victoria shooed them off, but at the moment, I didn't care. I watched the musical transform, like Mrs. Short said it would. The actors shined like a holly-wood star, while my own star collapsed in endless space. The props that took days or weeks to paint by hand, the only paint I painted was pitch black on my white canvas. The dancers stepped into their precise move-ments, but I danced into a depression phase. The musical harmonies that played were beautiful, however, my harmony hit a low note. Our experienced director who had a smile on her face, well, I'm a director for the musical of heartbreak. Finally, the first night arrived.

"We should have a sleepover tomorrow night, after the play," Aneska texted. The Wolves probably set her up to do this, to spy on me, and to get the inside information.

"Why?"

"I want to get to know you Minnie! This isn't anything having to do with The Wolves, and if you are wondering, than no, The Wolves didn't set me up, I do not want to spy on you, or get the inside information," Aneska insisted.

"Okay..." I responded, with a huge hesitation.

After putting my phone away, I proceeded to the unoccupied hallway, and dropped my bag. I leaned back in my chair and groaned like there is no tomorrow. Soon, the vacant hallway turned into crowds of actors, actresses, props, and when Clevis walked through the door, drama filled the empty hallway. I stared at him, like it is the first time I saw his true self. Clevis is glowing like an animated jellyfish, lighting up the depths of the ocean. He is the first colored photograph, staring in the first motion picture. A blue snowflake landing in a field of pearly white, or a rose in a sunflower garden, or the pillow in the pile of blan-kets. Is he those things though? I turned away from him.

The Wolves followed him, except for Aneska, who came over to Coraline and I. "Why aren't you with the pack?" Coraline snapped, with an eye roll.

"I... I mean... I guess I just want to hang out with you nerds," Aneska said. *Something strange is definitely going on. First, she invites me to sleepover, and now this, asking if she could be with Coraline and I. I would sincerely be surprised if she asked me to be her maid of honor, and with the direction this is going in, that would be possible.*

"Go back to your pack Aneska. We don't want you here, besides, don't you barge into our lives enough already?" Coraline grunted.

"Coraline! That is rude, Aneska can stay," I defended.

"Fine... so... Aneska... have you robbed a bank yet? I always wondered how much money you've stolen! I can contact Guinness World Records if you broke a record!" *I nudged Coraline and told her to shut up.*

"I won't brag of how many records I shattered, but I don't want to be treated like this, and Wolf or not, I'm still a person," Aneska snapped.

While they continued to argue, I sat down and looked at Clevis. I gazed at him, and he peered back at me, but then he turned away again.

"Are you okay?" Aneska asked.

"I have been better."

"You sure?"

"Yes," I assured. *If Aneska can't see through this, than that just shows I'm a good actor. Besides, that is what drama club is all about!*

Mrs. Short brought us together. *I spotted Clevis trying to avoid us, but he tripped over a costume. This is not Clevis' best day ever, like he said it would be when we were together. I did feel bad for him, but Clevis hit me with an ice spell. As cold as I am, tonight's focus is on Frozen, where magic comes to life.*

"Let me start off by saying, opening night is the most nerve wracking, mistakes in every scene, and there aren't many crowds. I want every single one of you to know that you have an important part in this completed project. We need to work together to make this a great experience, so that it isn't full of errors. This is my last year as a drama club director. I want it to be the best, and as I said in December, I know in my frozen heart that we'll all remember tonight, tomorrow, and our biggest show, on Saturday night!!" Mrs. Short exclaimed.

Everybody applauded, even The Wolves, who clapped, but rolled their eyes to look cool. Victoria squealed in her Elsa costume, making the other Wolves howl. After Mrs. Moon surveyed her sing in Science that time we had to sing about the planets, she told Mrs. Short about Victoria's voice. And the next thing we know, Victoria is the lead role.

Before I knew it, Coraline and I are silently jumping in our ensemble snowflake costumes. In a few seconds, that ruby red curtain will burst open, and myself, Coraline, and fifteen other people will flow like the snowflakes we are. Singing our hearts out, dancing our precise dance moves, and being as white as a snowflake. I have only been on stage a few times, whether it was for a school play, or an awards ceremony, or I felt like I was on stage when I had to participate in class. The only other time I was on stage was when I took theater camp. I was a detective dog, so the only lines I had was, woof. It was an intense part, at least for myself.

Despite the fact I had whiskers and fur, I felt needed and important then, like the time I discerned the first snowflake in Mrs. Moon's science room. I remember it like it was yesterday. Brightness filled the whole room, like heaven was flying through the windows. There, I saw something, something microscopic only as far the eye can see. Something with pattern and crystallized holes on the sides, something making me gleam. Something that reminded me of the time that I cut out paper snowflakes for Christmas last year. Then, I realized exactly what I was staring at. There, the first snowflake of winter, trickling to the ground, than being the person I was, I somehow compared a snowflake to the personality of Clevis Cleveland.

Snowflakes of all different shapes and sizes, like big, small, snazzy, short, tall, pretty, petty, fresh, frenzy, snow. Snowflakes are like people. All diverse, unique, and Clevis is a special snowflake. A loud snowflake, an obnoxious snowflake, or, a snowflake with many divergent textures... I liked it.

Now I looked at him once again. He is dressed up like a snowflake, and he looked noisy, annoying, and he added many textures to his costume. It stood out against the rest of the snowflakes... I loved that. But then, I glimpsed beyond the snowflake, to the coldness beneath it. Being the person I am, and being the way I am, I never could've seen it. Behind the snowflake, is the real Clevis, who has true feelings, and who is as hurt as I am.

All of a sudden, the curtain burst forth like an explosion, to reveal a full room of the gleaming audience. Our harmonious tones echoed off the outer walls, spreading to everyone. To sing "Let it Go", means to let go of your fears, and false hopes. To be known on stage, which is an amazing feeling to be felt. To let go of your memories, to let go of the people you love, and to let go what is hurting inside. I sang louder than the rest of the ensemble, even Victoria, like it is a battle of the bands. I croaked the words, but I squawked them with passion. I felt like my own snowflake, gleaming, outshining, and beautiful, like how a snowflake is supposed to be.

Frozen, Night Two

"CORALINE, GIVE ME MY HAT BACK!"

Clevis chased Coraline through the hallway like a wild goose chase through the woods of drama. I walked behind them, barely watching, like I'm hiding behind a tree. Coraline dodged props and costumes and people as she raced away from Clevis. They flew into the cafeteria where Clevis melodramatically huffed and puffed, than collapsed on the ground. That is a very Clevis thing to do.

Mrs. Short swiftly released a few papers and bolted to Clevis. She dropped to the floor and pretended to give him CPR. She pushed down on his chest several times, until he pretended to come back to life. This is why I love drama club.

"   What are you doing..." Clevis said, waking up from his endless slumber.

"What's going on here?!" Mrs. Short panicked.

"SHE TOOK MY HAT."

Coraline clenched it and stepped a few steps back. She covered her face in shame, and I slapped my forehead. Of course something like this happens... it always does.

"Coraline, give back his hat. I don't have time for this. We're putting on a show in a half hour and everyone is stressed. Just be nice to each other, just for tonight, please," Mrs. Short rebuked, trying to resist yelling. Coraline dropped it and apologized. Clevis snatched it from the floor and ran for his life.

They say that even though you may be the hero in your own story, you could also be the enemy in somebody else's. Clevis bolted away like Coraline and I are his arch-nemesis', and before scampering from the room, he looked at me like I'm his murderer.

Well, welcome to night two of Center Middle School's Frozen. The night didn't start well, and before that whole scene happened, I tried to avoid Clevis as best as possible. Until Coraline caused another mischief action, I was calm, collected, and content. She just had to go over there and take his snowflake hat. And the next thing I know, the only thing I looked forward to is the sleepover with Aneska, and that is a surprising thing to be excited about. I would rather be at Aneska's house trying to make small talk instead of here, getting yelled at by Mrs. Short fifteen minutes before the school play.

I can only imagine what Aneska planned in her mind, and I wondered what The Wolves did at previous sleepovers. They probably do manicures and pedicures, or gossip about the latest gossip, or perhaps they create a burn book to roast the unpopular people at this school. Or, perhaps they toilet papered the governor's house, or with all the money Victoria owns, they probably took an overnight trip to Paris.

I found Aneska putting on makeup after the second show ended. Even though the musical is over for tonight, and loads of people are washing off makeup, Aneska smeared lipstick on her lips and applied more mascara. She brushed and curled her hair as though she got nominated for an Emmy Award. In my opinion, she looks like a diva, a younger version of Lady Gaga.

"I have to look good for the public," She complained.

"Aneska, this is the east coast. You don't need to look perfect," I insisted. She chuckled and put away her makeup, which I never thought she'd do. She showed me her limousine after we walked out of the school. All adults and children are staring in awe as Aneska gestured me inside.

"This is just a gift Victoria gave me for my birthday," She replied. "Besides, you know how wealthy she is."

She leaned back and pretended to be a boss, putting sunglasses on. We talked about our school lives, and what our plans are for the summer, and Clevis didn't pop up at all. We drove by the beach and decided to take a pit stop. Aneska is prepared by bringing a large quilt, which had an ancient theme to it. The warm April weather is beautiful tonight, so I left my coat in the limo and let myself breathe the cool salt air. The moonlight reflected off the ocean and the sand. I took my shoes off and my toes played with the sand. The shells scraping against my feet weren't sharp, and I laid down on Aneska's quilt, savoring the sound of the waves crashing. Aneska sat down beside me, and I nudged her.

"Thanks for doing this. I usually don't hang out with too many people,"
I sighed. She nudged me back, and bits of sand floated into my hair.

"Same here Minnie. We both have our issues," She said. "How are
things with Clevis?"

I was the bearer of bad news when I told her.

"You two lovebirds are having problems?!" She threw sand at me
and screamed. "Wait... wait.. No... no... this isn't possible... couples
counseling... WHAT HAPPENED?!?!"

She grasped on me and demanded me to tell her.

I told her the whole story, adding how she decided to stay out of it.

"I think I should talk to him tomorrow night, because that is the
last night of the play, and after that, is a week long school vacation. It
is only right that we break up or not," I lamented. My hand played with
the sand, and I looked to the water. I'm closer to the abyss, deep water
is a foot away from me.

"Minnie, that is a great idea. I'm going to be a good friend by telling you that it isn't right to be playing with Clevis like he's an object.
But still... I can't believe nobody told me about this," She said, astounded. "I feel like.. like.. like I'm not popular anymore," She sobbed. I put
my hand on her shoulder.

"Well, there are things that are more important than popularity.
Not many people knew. For that matter, you don't NEED to know
EVERYTHING about our relationship. Because the truth is, you and
The Wolves have been pressuring A LOT in the past few weeks, and if
you are a true friend, than you wouldn't build me like a sandcastle with
water running against it."

Aneska nodded and leaned against me.

"Victoria can create a lot of pressure, because she's a supermodel, a
rich child, she's on the cover of several magazines. She's like, my idol,
and one of my best friends... but not so much anymore. I don't feel in-

cluded in The Wolves... I'm not popular... and at the same time, I think I
would be happier being your friend, even if you're slightly less famous.
I'm sorry if I'm ever mean to you, or if I'm the water running against
your sand castle," Aneska apologized. She sobbed on my shoulder, like
the dramatic wolf she is, or perhaps, she's the person who is forced to
become a wolf at a full moon. I gazed at the moon reflecting our ocean,
than I stared at the person Aneska truly is.

Frozen, Night Three.

I was in tears by the time the last show ended. Besides, anything
that comes to an end is upsetting. All good things come to a conclu-
sion at some point, even if the good things are great, and even if the
great things are greater, or even if the greater things are greatest. All the
greatest things come to an ending, even the drama club for this year.

"Hi Mrs. Short. It's the final night," I sighed.

"At the end of tonight and knowing me, I will probably be in tears,
being director and all."

Her eyes are already a bit watery, and so are mine. I was talking
with Aneska last night about this, and it at that moment it dawned on me
that tonight is it.

"You were a great director, always telling us to focus and pay attention, and I apologize if I didn't do that all the time."

"I bet you had a fun time at couples counseling. Yes Minnie, I know
about that, and so does everybody else. But remember, if you wanted
to focus on this extracurricular activity, you could've said no to them.
You're a unique kid, as I heard. You deserved to be treated better in
this club. As for tonight, stay with your true friends, and ignore The
Wolves," She said. I thanked her and she patted my back.

For the last time, I walked into the hallway and put my bag down. I
sighed and took a seat in the metal chair I set up previous days ago, one
last time. Coraline also sat next to me, and exhaled, one last time.

"Man, I'm gonna to miss this, even the couples counseling. We had so many amazing memories in this club. Min, favorite memory?" She asked. There are so many memories to savor, which is the thing I wanted most in drama club. When Coraline told Clevis I had a crush on him, or, when Clevis got me the almond chocolate. The couples counseling thing, then there is the musical in general. That joyous feeling you get on stage, where you're meant to be. And you can find true passion just by being superior to everyone else on that wooden stage floor. This whole encounter has been a real experience, with all the definitions of drama. Being dramatic, participating in drama club, and drama in general. I answered Coraline's question with another.

"What isn't my favorite memory Coraline? For every moment I spent here, with my drama club family, it has been worthwhile, and good or bad, I still got the drama experience" I said to Coraline, and to Aneska who joined us. We smiled at each other, in the blink of an eye.

The final show ended it in the wink of an eye. As soon as it came, it came. I found myself bowing on stage, for the last time. I smiled and sighed with relief, until a shadow stirred. Clevis lurked in the corner, pacing back and forth. I have to talk to him now. It is now, or never. He is hurting, and with myself being different, that couldn't come in the way of how he is distressing.

People are blurs, and my eyes are only set on Clevis. I felt like I'm walking in slow motion. He puffed heavily, and looked at me like I am the abyss he fell into. We descended hard, and deep, and with me being special, I couldn't have the brain to know that. Like Mrs. Short said, we both have roles when it comes to the importance of a relationship. With everything I've been through, he has also been through. When he said he admired me, I said I adored him. He said he loved me to the moon, and to the sun, and I told him I idolized him throughout the rest of space. We were both loved, hated, hurting, and it is because of a seating chart I am autistic about. I hurt the both of us without realizing it.

"Minnie... I do love you, but, I don't think this will work."

This is the most quiet thing he's ever said. When I say he said it, he said it very softly, like a tiny asteroid traveling through the universe, and hitting earth so hard, crushing my world and spirit. The owl inside of me flew away from my broken world. He embraced me for the last time, and is crying too. He cried on my shoulders, but neither of us cared. Drama club wouldn't be the same without us together. We held hands and bowed one last time. Our relationship might've not worked now, but the memories will last a lifetime. I knew it in my heart, but only, it is gone.

Chapter 10

"Oh... so glum... so tired... so done with life... what a tragedy... vacation is over... oh so gloom... so gloom... so groan... so growl... it's over... WAKE UP!" Mrs. Moon exclaimed. Everybody jerked their skulls up after staring into space.

"Welcome back, and happy Monday to all. First off, great job to anybody who participated in the musical. That was a hoot! Frozen the movie, as a play. That film cannot be more popular. So, I know we're tired, it's first period, our sleep schedules are messed up, but I have a surprise for you... a project presentation counting for an exam grade!" Mrs. Moon gushed. Nowadays, the only thing that mattered about this is the seating chart for it. We've had no seating chart since Valentine's Day, that unspeakable day. Even after Mrs. Moon was about to assign a new seating chart, and Clevis shouted out his love for me in front of the entire class, Mrs. Moon "forgot" about the arrangement. That is a classic two birds with one stone. Recently, I just gained the courage to make eye contact with Mrs. Moon again. Three birds with one stone!

"Today, I am going to introduce the solar system project. This will be a major assessment grade, and a national science exam grade, so we will be working on this for the rest of the year. Your group will choose a planet to study deeply about, than you'll make a presentation to share with the class. You will be looking at the amount of gases on that planet, how it affects the solar system, the shape, size, temperature, among many other things on the rubric. Since we'll be working on this for everyday for the next two months, I want you to put in your best effort. I expect a great presentation," Mrs. Moon informed. She explained the project in detail, taking up half of the period.

"Okay... now for your ASSIGNED groups," She started...

The lonely desks looked back at us. I leaned against the wall, and dread split over me like spilled water on my sketchbook. A new seating chart is any student's worst nightmare, to a person like me.

As Mrs. Moon walked to the back of the room, and the tension grew like a building wave crushing upon the innocent sand below. She faced the back row, with her teacher's pointer finger out and ready to fire.

Imagine yourself in the climax of a movie, with the antagonist rising. I'm the protagonist, in agonising pain, Mrs. Moon controlling it. The smirk on her face made me want to crumple like a piece of paper. I stared at the last three people left. Clevis, the distracting and somewhat demented class clown, and to Coraline, the goth girl with FAILING grades. I gulped, glancing at the last open seats. Well, I lived a good fourteen years.

"Coraline, Clevis, and let's put Minnie in the middle!" Mrs. Moon exclaimed. While the science class is on Earth, myself, Coraline, and Clevis are on another planet. Now, and forever, I am in the back row, with two monkeys sitting right and left of me. I'm a lone wolf.

I'm just the girl in the middle.

Every time Mrs. Moon mentions a seating chart, or wants another seating chart, this moment repeatedly plays in my head over and over again. The tension is always spilling over me like spilled water on my sketchbook. But then, the moment I dreaded most of all finally arrived.

"For your assigned seating chart... it will be those groups I put you into in December."

I knew better, so I smiled... but I covered that fact that HOLY MOTHER OF TOMATO PLANTS. WHAT IS SHE DOING TO ME... SHE KNOWS WE GOT TOGETHER AND I DUMPED HIM AND WE GOT BACK AND BROKE UP AGAIN. SHE KNEW ABOUT THE PRESSURE FROM The Wolves AND MY PROBLEMS WITH THIS SEATING CHART.... AHHHHHHH (F word) MRS. MOON.

As I walked to the back row, I smiled, like nothing ever happened.

"Friendly group, for the next month until school ends, our focus will be on THIS project, and nothing else. There will be no 'couples counseling', or 'drama', or 'anything else'. The Wolves already did their worst, so we're going to do our best to ignore them," I stated. I grabbed a paper from Mrs. Moon, and started reading it, ignoring Coraline and Clevis' expressions.

"Minnie's taking a dictatorship," Clevis complained.

"I'm just stating the FACTS Clevis." Clevis snatched the page and held it away from me. I tried reaching for it, but Clevis hide it away. I'm the new Coraline by starting a fight with him, and that never happened before. Mrs. Moon rushed over, and gave the three of us separate papers. Nice going Mrs. Moon. Two thumbs up.

Welcome to your planet choices. You and your group will select one planet to further your research in. Here are a few details about each of the planet's and solar system features we know of. Remember to choose wisely, as this is what you'll be studying for the rest of the year.

Mercury: the smallest and innermost planet in the Solar System. Its orbital period around the Sun of 87.97 days is the shortest of all the planets in the Solar System. It is named after the Roman deity Mercury, the messenger of the gods.

Venus: The second planet from the Sun, orbiting it every 224.7 Earth days. It has the longest rotation time of any planet in the Solar

System and rotates in the opposite direction to most other planets. It does not have any natural satellites.

Mars: The fourth planet from the Sun and the second-smallest planet in the Solar System after Mercury.

Jupiter: The fifth planet from the Sun and the largest in the Solar System. It is a gigantic planet with a mass one-thousandth that of the Sun, but two-and-a-half times that of all the other planets in the Solar System combined.

Saturn: The sixth planet from the Sun and the second-largest in the Solar System, after Jupiter. It is a gas giant with an average radius about nine times that of Earth.

Uranus: The seventh planet from the Sun. It has the third-largest planetary radius and fourth-largest mass in the Solar System.

Neptune: The eighth and farthest planet from the Sun in the Solar System. In the Solar System, it is the fourth largest planet by diameter, the third-most-massive planet, and the densest giant planet.

Earth's Moon: The Moon, of course, has been known since prehistoric times. It is the second brightest object in the sky after the Sun. As the Moon orbits around the Earth once per month, the angle between the Earth, the Moon and the Sun changes; we see this as the cycle of the Moon's phases.

The Sun: The star at the center of the Solar System. It is a nearly a sphere of hot plasma, with internal convective motion that generates a magnetic field via a dynamo process.

"Let's do the sun. Easy A I presume," Coraline mentioned.

"I think we should do the moon!!!!" Clevis said.

"Let's do a planet. We don't know much about them and it would be cool to learn about it. Even though they may not seem easy, it is worth it to make our own discoveries about them," I persuaded.

"The Sun, because--."

"The moon, it's really awesome," Clevis clamoured.

The sun and moon are opposites, just like Clevis and Coraline. Those opposites are trying to take the spotlight from each other, with every day and night passing. It's a constant battle between the Coraline, the gigantic sun full of gases, and to Clevis, the smaller object in the sky, the rock that tries to control the waves. I'm the Earth that is in the middle, silently watching them revolve around me, again and again and again and again.

"Why all the bickering back row?" Mrs. Moon asked. I held my breath.

"SHE DUMPED ME IN FRONT OF THE WHOLE---"

"Not true. You tried to cheat with---," I said, more heartbroken.

"THAT WAS A MISTAKE---," Clevis admitted.

"Really Clevis? It was a mistake to wander off with another girl, blush at her, hold her hand, and say, 'Jill, I like you. I'm not sure about Minnie.'"

"I can't believe I loved you once..."

There it is. The elephant in the room just jumped out the window, breaking the wall. I felt like the building collapsed on me, like a piles of brick hitting my head. I fell unconscious of my surroundings, into a deep, black abyss, failing like the black heart I consumed.

"Start focusing on your work or else I'll give the whole back row detention."

Mrs. Moon stormed away, sat in her desk, and glared at the three of us. Three thumbs up for you Mrs. Moon!

"The moon," Coraline quietly said.

"Fine."

"Yes!"

"Time's up! Now let's agree on who is doing which feature in the solar system. Who wants to do Uranus?" Mrs. Moon shouted, as A LOT of people raised their hands. A group got that one.

"Jupiter?"

A group got that one.

"Pluto? Ah, trick question, that isn't considered a planet. How about the Sun?"

Five groups lifted their hands. Coraline shot hers up, and I gently placed my hand on her elbow and brought it down. She moaned and banged her head on the desk.

"Now, who wants to do the Moon?" Mrs. Moon queried. Nobody elevated their hands, some people even looked down. Clevis stood up, jumped up and down, and flashed his hand into the air. Coraline didn't raise hers at all.

"Do all of you agree on it?" Mrs. Moon asked. Clevis shouted yes and she looked at me for clarification. I nodded and gave her my approval. The moon is ours, with the back row group, for a national exam grade. Many more battles will come between our group, like eclipses, revolutions, and solely trying to take the spotlight.

My homeroom teacher asked me to run an errand today. A simple task, bringing a note to Mrs. Moon. I took it with care, walked to the science hallway with caution, and opened Mrs. Moon's door. In her room are The Wolves and Clevis, and they are sitting together, probably gossiping about me. I rushed the message to Mrs. Moon, gave it to her, and right before my errand is complete, I hear my name pop up. Several times actually, like popcorn popping in the hot microwave. I'm about to be roasted, than I'll burn from being overheated.

"Clevis, I heard about you and Minnie. And I, Victoria, am very sorry for you. But you two lovebirds did love each other once, so why not again? You should get back together with Minnie."

Not a surprise I walked into this, but what makes it more awkward is how Jill is sitting right next to Clevis. If I'm in this homeroom, I would've switched out on the first day of school.

"I hate her!!!"

Victoria sneered, and I did also.

"Well, I don't think Clevis and I will be getting BACK TOGETH-ER. We ALL know that HE has a CRUSH on JILL," I exclaimed. So do you know how someone can foolishly blurt out something by accident? Like an answer to an easy question, or a secret you've blown? A secret that you don't even realize that you blurted to your friend? Well, I just divulged out something that made me feel all the guilt in the world. I revealed Clevis' crush to the whole class. All the culpability in the world laid upon me, piled on me, set on me, like I'm holding the world on my bare two hands. 13,170 sextillion pounds.

Mrs. Moons homeroom jerked their heads up to see me at the door, half open, one foot out. Victoria smirked like she adored this kind of drama. Mrs. Moon crossed her arms, mouthing, "What the hell did you just do?!". The room is silent. I only listened to the water running through the pipes. I listened to my imaginary screams as I fell into my visual abyss. I screamed and screeched like water running against rusted metal. The owl I imagined had disappointment etched on her wise face, and she wouldn't save me from falling. I descended into eternal dark-ness, with not a light in sight. It is because of an errand, a simple task my homeroom teacher asked me to do.

Tears streamed down Clevis' face and he ran, almost tripping over his seat. He flashed past me, gasping, "what kind of a monster are you," and he slammed the door, covering his crying face.

"Back to reality everyone. I don't want another word, or blurt, out of any of you," Mrs. Moon scolded. I bolted out the door, hearing only whispers about our relationship. More guilt spilled over me like water to a shower, and it is so bad that soap got into my eyes and they stung. My eyes sting in real life.

The only person who is proud is Coraline. When I told her at lunch that very same day, she laughed and clapped her hands like an innocent baby seal.

"This is nothing to be happy over," I breathed.

"Are you kidding? This is the best news I've heard all day! I never knew you could be a BTS, a baddy two shoes."

"It just blurted out, like after a snap of the finger, I realized what I said. Then, I felt bad, like all the guilt in the world laid upon me," I cried. She patted my back and her bony skin leaned against my BTS body.

"I am a horrible person."

"You shouldn't. It was a mistake, and we've all made huge mistakes like that."

"I guess so... we have Science last period... with Clevis," I moaned.

"I heard we have a substitute teacher in that class," Coraline mentioned.

"Weird, Mrs. Moon was here this morning. I remember her snarling at me as though I'm a troublemaker."

"Well, if there is a sub, we should talk to him about it. Mrs. Moon lessens the awkwardness between you and Clevis, because for the past couple of weeks, he's been able to sit away from us. I'm very surprised Mrs. Moon hasn't changed the groups. However, this substitute doesn't have experience with our... situation," Coraline said. I agreed with her, and we concurred to confront the substitute.

When we walked into Science, the subs snarly face snarled more as
he took a seat at Mrs. Moon's desk. I gestured Coraline to go, and her
legs are shaking as she approached the most spiteful substitute in the
whole school district. He growled at her, and put his nasty feet on the
table. Coraline doesn't have a pleasant history with substitutes, particularly that one.

"Hi..."

The substitute groaned.

"As you know, I'm Coraline, you know me, the goody two shoes
of this class. In the back of the room is Minnie, the person with long
brownish-blackish hair, blue eyes, a very cheesy face, the one who is
waving at us right now. Now that I nicely introduced us decent fellows,
I would like to request that one of our group members, Clevis, sit away
from us. We've gotten into some conflicts with him in the past, and so
I wouldn't like to cause any trouble for you," Coraline informed, in the
nicest tone she's ever talked in.

"It is true," I continued. "We communicate through email. He can
be in the empty front row desk, and that way, we'll have peace with
each other."

The substitute nodded his head. "Is this the kid who's a disruption
to the class?" he cackled. My palms felt sweaty and my face burned up.

"Maybe?"

"Aren't you the girl..." he started.

"Nope!"

"Fine, you can sit away from him."

With his permission engraved in my mind, I moved my feet to
move farther away from him. Coraline and I politely ran back to our
seats and Clevis sneered at me. Remembering what I did to him earlier,
I bluntly let Coraline do the talking.

"Clevis, you can sit in that empty desk in the front row. I already got permission from the substitute," Coraline demanded. He moved away in a heartbeat, other people staring at us.

Somehow, this spread around the school in less than five hours. I got called some nasty things earlier, and I am those. I'm like the Grinch on Christmas because not only did I steal all the presents and Christmas decorations, but I also caused a blizzard on Christmas. I am a storm, storming on everyone's happy life, like Clevis' for instance.

We continued to work on the presentation. When I say "we", I meant that I worked on it. Clevis is playing games, and Coraline is looking up song lyrics. I got the opportunity to design the cover page! And everything else after that.

Soon after I finished the cover to our PowerPoint, Coraline accidentally copied and pasted some lyrics on it. The lyrics in there is from the famous song, Hallelujah. She put it next to Clevis' name.

"Your faith was strong but you needed proof,

You saw her bathing on the roof,

Her beauty and the moonlight overthrew you,

She tied you to her kitchen chair,

She broke your throne and she cut your hair,

And from your lips she drew the Hallelujah..."

"DELETE THAT RIGHT NOW!!!!"

Coraline copied and pasted lyrics, and when Clevis thought she is referring to me. How he must've seen the lyrics to have the biggest reaction;

"My faith was strong but I needed proof,

You saw Minnie bathing on the roof,

Her beauty and the moonlight overthrew me,

Minnie tied you to her kitchen chair,

Minnie broke your throne and she cut your hair,

And from my lips Minnie drew the Hallelujah..."

Coraline tried to delete it as fast as the pointer can take her. This moment must be as rare as a lightning bolt striking on me. How Clevis is paying attention at the exact moment Coraline is on the document. It's an eclipse happening, when the moon is blocking out the sun, making the whole Earth filled with darkness at every lyric.

"WHY ARE YOU TWO SO MEAN?!?!?" Clevis bawled. His laptop smashed and crashed on the floor, and his face boiled and fists clenched from throwing it. He is a storm that got bigger and larger, until the winds started. He slammed the door on the way out, causing a tsunami. Rain poured on my head, I'm all wet. I am soaked with guilt.

"It was just song lyrics..." Coraline whispered. The whole class heard her whisper, because it is silent. A quiet storm arose, commenced, and is in play.

I deleted the song lyrics myself.

For one week, it has been downright strange between Clevis and I. The class was signifying a change of mood having to do with the incident on April 14th. Clevis throwing his laptop on the ground, storming out of the room, and according to most people in our science class, he's never been more angry. Even The Wolves were hushed, in fact, they were hiding like typical wolves at a new moon. Ever since then, Clevis has been acting strange.

In the hallway before walking into Science that next Monday, Clevis' face was blotchy and he pushed right past me. He stomped into Science and slammed the door in my face. When I walked in, he set his head on the desk and moaned. He didn't shout out, or make any comments to anything, in fact, he was the most silent student that day. Even more surprisingly, he DID HIS WORK. To a usual person, that would be normal, but to be somebody like Clevis, I consider that abnormal. He's always nervous coming into school, then after lunch, his face would be blotchy, like he's been crying. For the rest of the day after that, he would remain silent. Coraline noticed a difference, and she asked him if he was okay. He nodded his head, avoiding eye contact.

"Wow Coraline, are you turning over a new leaf? I've never seen you concerned or worried for Clevis," I whispered a few days later.

"He has been acting really strange. Just want to make sure he's alright, for working on the project, you know?"

I nodded my head. The back row is slowly improving. Clevis isn't talking, and Coraline likes the quiet. We quietly worked on the slide-show together. Mrs. Moon assigned us different things to research so we have been occupied.

When Mrs. Moon came back, the substitute didn't tell her anything, so throughout this week, she's been trying to learn about what happened last Friday. "Minnie... so... did anything between this group happen when I was absent?" She asked. I shrugged.

"Not really Mrs. Moon," I said, and nothing more after that.

But overall, as the final weeks of school approached, we worked on our projects, The Wolves calmed down, but there is still something wrong with Clevis. It was late at night when I decided, this has gone too far. I grew up learning not to meddle, but I am now meddling, because for one, I need to see what's the matter with Clevis, and two, I should apologize to him. I whipped out my phone and texted Clevis. He didn't respond. I facetimed him. He didn't answer. I texted him again saying this is important. He didn't retort. I called him again. He didn't rejoin. I did it again, and again, and one more time.

He finally picked up in tears. His face is blotchy, and there are red rashes around his black eyes. He is sweating and his eyebrows are low. His eyelashes are wet like the dripping icicles off my roof. Clevis wouldn't stop sniffling

"Are you okay??"

"Obviously, not."

"You need to tell me what's wrong."

"Hunter is being mean to me," he said.

"I know that Hunter is a nasty kid, but what is he doing to you to make you this upset?"

"When I sit at my lunch table, he calls me bad words. He always makes fun of me, and makes me want to kill myself! He always makes fun of me and Jill... ever since YOU revealed my crush. It makes me so mad at what he says and does. I just want to punch him in the face. The more angry I am at him, the more I want to fight him. I know I can't though, because he is way stronger. I set up a battle for lunch tomorrow, and I'm nervous about it. He called you seaweed, and called me a shrimp. We are sea organisms!!!"

I got called seaweed. That is concerning since I have no similarities with that plant. And more worrying, Clevis is being bullied.

"Clevis, this is not okay. You're getting hurt, and I'm going to be a good ex-girlfriend by saying this. You can't fight him, as much you want to, you just can't. You will be in so much trouble, you would get a detention, suspension, or, you could be expelled! It could ruin your life, forever," I warned him. I don't want him to have a worse reputation than now. He'll lose the fight because unlike him, Hunter has muscle. "I don't care if I'm in trouble," Clevis stammered.

"Well Clevis, I won't let it happen. Fighting and violence is always the wrong option. Remember all those presentations from elementary school about non-violence? Listen to that. First, I want you to make things right with Hunter, and perhaps he'll apologize. Next, come to a new lunch table, you can sit with Coraline and I if you want. Third, if this continues to bother you, than tell a teacher," I ordered. "Also, to make you a little better now, I want to say sorry for everything I have done to you. It was not right for me to treat you like an object, and I'm not sure if you knew this, but I have a special condition that makes my brain wired in a different way. But I can only blame myself for the events that happened, and Mrs. Moon for creating that nasty seating chart." He nodded and accepted my apology.

After that, I hung up and went on a search to find Hunter's number. Now, this is meddling. Clevis doesn't deserve this. He didn't deserve me, he deserves a life without anybody taunting him, or dating him for the attention of it.

"Dearest Hunter, this is somebody texting you to inform you that Clevis wants to fight you. That concerns me, because apparently, you are being mean to him? I want you to STOP, put yourself in his shoes and maybe you can see that he is really upset. Thank you, but not thank you. -Seaweed"

I strapped on my white high heels, and gazed into the mirror. Besides seeing a girl in a short white dress, I see a woman who saved the day. In that mirror, I glimpsed at the makeup on my face, but the only making up Clevis has to do is to thank me for saving him. In this mirror, I see a white purse with my phone and money in it. The white bag had golden chains on it, and I'm hoping to not create a black chain of drama tonight. In that mirror, I caught sight of a fierce and strong single woman, wishing for a miracle that this night goes well.

This has been a good day, one of those good days I don't have very often. At lunch today, when the fight is supposed to happen, I sat at a table with a good view. Clevis is acting like himself, but his left foot is moving back and forth. That is how I know he's nervous, and he is as anxious as a person about to stand up to a bully. Finally, Hunter approached him. Clevis put down his sandwich with a suspicious look. I watched as Hunter's lip moved and Clevis nodded. I will never know if Clevis knows I texted Hunter. I'm not going to tell him. I'll let him be satisfied with himself. Because, do you know what? I am a fine piece of seaweed.

In the mirror, there is seaweed. Hunter tried to eat me, but to his chubby self, I'm too strong for his taste buds. A few minutes ago, Clevis called to thank me for influencing him to stop the fight. Now, we are friends, and only friends. Tonight will be a good night, filled with friends, and only friends.

From what I've heard and seen, school dances break hearts. With a dance, at least one person ends up crying, and yet, we all keep on going back. Hopefully, I can get this night over with, because next week, we have finals testing for four days, and I hear our teachers have a surprise in store for us. I'm hoping to have middle school over with so I will never see The Wolves again, or Clevis, or Coraline, or Mrs. Moon.

Once I arrived, there are The Wolves in their fancy dresses and taking selfies. Then there is Clevis wandering awkwardly around that group. Speaking of the geeks, people are reading at the tables that are set up. The goth blend in with the darkness, and the musical people are playing around with the DJ. Everybody is in there certain groups, and I finally found mine on the dancing floor.

For this dance, there are two main rooms. The gym, and the cafeteria. The gym is the dance room, with blasting music and beaming lights. In the cafeteria, is a photo booth, the snack sales, and the ticket collections. In between them, is a very crowded hallway. There are more than three hundred students here, so it is quite busy.

Coraline came to me, said hello, and I nearly fainted at her appearance. She looked like the opposite of her usual self, by dressing in all pink, and BRUSHING HER HAIR. She looked like a princess who rides a motorcycle. She also wore a bucket load of makeup, which does not suit her well. "Minnie! I'm glad you decided to come!" Coraline said, in a british accent.

"What the hell happened to you?"

"Well honey bunny, I turned over a new leaf. And now, let's find you a new date" She said. "Cheerio!"

"Wait! I'm perfectly fine as single as a pringle!" I yelled, but Coraline ran around like a Victoria, trying to find me someone to dance with. I promised myself that tonight, I will not meddle with things. I will not dance with any boys (except Rogelio if that miracle happens). I will be The Statue of Liberty, still like a statue, but I will create freedom and make people feel good about themselves. And that will happen with my silence.

As I walked around, watching my peers talk, and laugh, I felt like a girl. Not necessary a girl in the middle, but more of a girl along the outskirts, wanting to dance in the middle. A romantic song started playing, for the only slow dance of the night. Everybody partnered up, and the lights are dim. I stared off into the distance, seeing Clevis dancing with Jill. They just blended in The Wolves crowd, and I am once again, like before the seating chart, alone, and wanting more. Clevis and his tuxedo, and Jill with her long flowery purple dress. Their arms are wrapped around one another, both blushing and smiling with pearly white teeth. Clevis got his braces off. They are made for each other, and like I said before, dances break hearts.

The cafeteria is like a freezer compared to the gym. Chills went down my spine as I left, and my head felt cold once I slumped in the cafeteria. I'm in there alone, except, a shadow stirred, and Rogelio sat at the other side of the room. He's seated on one of the benches, with nobody else in sight. The lights in the cafeteria are dim, while my heart lit up.

"Are you okay Rogelio?" I asked, compassionately. He leaned up against me, and I felt more heated than I did in the gym. We are friends, just friends, and only friends. I am the Statue of Liberty, silent, hesitant, but wanting more. More world peace, and less hurt in the world. I wanted a snowy owl to fly on my crown, and tell me everything will be okay. But that isn't possible right now, and it may never be, and that is the truth.

"I am sick to my stomach. I came here alone, and nobody came to me, or said hello. I want to go home, but you know what the rules state. We can't leave the building until the dance is over," He cried. He's having a worse night then me, and I'm having a pretty awful night. In my solid white dress, I felt 50 shades of gray. In Rogelio's black tuxedo, he felt merely black.

"It is alright Rogelio, because I feel the exact same way. Jill is dancing with Clevis. Even though we're broken up, it still feels kind of, hurtful," I confided. He nodded, and leaned his head on my shoulder. I felt a teardrop on my chest, just a single drop. A drop of out of a black heart, but a drop of golden bliss. Two hearts were torn tonight, and we were brought together. I consider that a miracle.

All of a sudden, I heard a light noise. I thought I'm going crazy until Rogelio lifted his head. The sound got louder... it almost sounded like the fire drill alarm. The music stopped playing, and only then did I know it is the alarm. I turned around to see everyone rushing and pushing each other to the door. Rogelio and I stuck together as we tried to bolt out of the school.

"Calm down!!!" The principal shouted over the microphone. Nobody listened to her over all the screaming. It is like the tiny orchestra in Titanic when the ship was sinking. They wouldn't stop playing until the last few seconds, but people just trampled it. Running for their dear lives, and indeed, the Titanic sank.

The dance is over, which signifies no more hearts can be broken. The building is close to being broken, because nobody knows why the fire alarm went off, or what will happen in the future. Facing our burning school, I squeezed Rogelio's hand as he leaned on me, softly whispering in my ear, that everything will be okay.

Chapter 11

Our school is in the course of burning flames. I watched the smoke escape from the windows as everybody gazed over the melting bricks of Center Middle School. Our school is burning from the heat everybody has given it, the coal everybody has tested on it, and in everybody's eyes, I saw the reflection of a fierce, daunting, flame. When our school burned down, that flame extinguished from peoples hearts, but unlike everybody else, my heart burned along with this school. Today, May 1st, the only feeling I had is my heart burning from the final exams we have to take.

"As you know, the teachers have been keeping a secret about our final exams. I am going to tell you what we're doing for the test. Instead of a typical paper and pencil test, myself, along with the rest of the teachers have decided to put you in groups. In your group, you will be creating a presentation on ANY topic, and we will all present them on the last day of school. School isn't just about academics and tests, but it's about learning about yourself as a person, so we're testing to see how you've improved yourself over the last year. We need you to be working productively and you will have twenty hours to work on these, so we expect a good show!" Mrs. Short explained.

My assigned teacher is Mrs. Moon, and my group is with Aneska and Coraline. Ever since Aneska opened up to me about Victoria, we

became our own wolf pack, by sticking together in Science, and standing up for each other. For this presentation, three is the perfect number.
Besides, three is the first number to which the meaning "all" was given.
It is The Triad, being the number of the whole as it contains the beginning, a middle and an end. The power of three is universal and is the
tripartite nature of the world as heaven, earth, and waters. It is human as
body, soul and spirit. Three is a powerful number, and we are going to
rock this presentation.

I found myself running down the hallway to Mrs. Moon's science
classroom, whipping the door open. Even though it was still a little
awkward between Mrs. Moon and I, she somehow heard about me
standing up to Hunter. And once again, she treated me like an angel
in Science. I blissfully sat in the front row with my group of three,
prepared for the best week of my life.

After I saw Clevis wander into the room, like a half-sleeping dwarf,
I prepared for the worst week of my life. He's assigned to the same
room, with me, for an entire week. Even though I helped him with
Hunter, I had a feeling our relationship will never be the same. As long
as The Wolves don't show up here, I think I can grab some wood, start
a fire, and survive in the wild. However, if the Wolves come in our way,
that fire can burn life, just like how they and Clevis will burn me, like
how I hoped the false fire could burn this school. He sat in the back row.
"Minnie, PAY ATTENTION," Coraline shouted.

"Sorry, sorry, so sorry," I mumbled, still staring at the back of the
room.

"What topic should we cover for the presentation?" she asked. We
looked at each other with different angles and expressions. We came
up with some weak ideas, like a presentation on dogs, or cats, global
warming, or even how to find a lost object. Everything was lost until
Rogelio strolled into the room in search of a group. He is a lost warrior

that will be heroic to save the powerful triangles social lives. There he is, my knight in shining armor, the one whose hands held mine during a burning catastrophe. I could write a fantasy novel out of this, or, I could write a romance manuscript.

"Mrs. Moon! I need a group! My other group kicked me out..." Rogelio grumbled. Clevis snarled at him. They act like sweethearts, but behind eachothers back, they despise each other. If they got put together in a seating chart, I'd watch them like it was a thriller movie. That would be a disturbing movie, so viewer discretion advised. I'm hoping one of them will leave the room before blood starts spilling everywhere.

"Rogelio, why don't you join Minnie's group?" Mrs. Moon suggested.

"Of course he can join us!"

Having Rogelio in my group for a whole week sounds like a fairytale coming to life, but him and I are friends, only friends, and friends is all we'll ever be. I pulled up an extra chair to make our triangle group into a square section. Number four is considered inauspicious in traditional Chinese feng shui because it sounds like "death" in Cantonese. It is not only in feng shui that the number 4 is considered unlucky, but since it's Rogelio who joined us, I consider myself very lucky.

"Rogelio, what do you think we should do for the presentation?" I questioned him.

"Let's do something with pizazz! Jazz hands!" He said, doing the jazz hands.

"What's something other people will be interested in?"

"Wait.." I brainstormed. "Let's do the significance of having a good relationship. I'm practically an expert in this subject, and I can give advice to everybody! With a tiny bit of humor," I suggested. The teachers didn't give us a limit of what we can talk about, besides, they said we can do ANY topic.

And the next thing I know, our group is telling Mrs. Moon about my brilliant and glorious idea. I have a list of arguments if she says no, but being the teacher she is, she'll allow it.

Before she could answer, the lunch bell rang. She laughed way too hard for it to be real, so I took it as a yes. It's like auditioning for a talent show. I have the best ideas and everyone who judges says yes, because I am simply talented. One day, I will win America's got Talent, but, in four and a half days, I'll be presenting a PowerPoint about my love life.

Later that night, I sat at my drawing desk in my room. This is the exact same place where I first asked Clevis to be my boyfriend, and this is also the place where he told me he wanted to be my future husband. I simply laughed at that memory, those were the good times. It was another study session before the geography bee, and it was after we had our first kiss. During that study session, he forced me to show him my drawers, to prove there wasn't any love notes from my former crushes. Instead, Clevis spotted a photo copy of everybody in our grade.

"Minnie, aren't you like amazing at drawing and art like that? If you drew this picture, then all the tiny people could look so awesome in a portrait. The school could be so impressed!! And maybe they'll hang it up!!!" He suggested, getting hyped at a huge project.

"Clevis, you know how busy I am. I haven't been drawing lately, I'm not sure why, well, I guess it's because I haven't been feeling the inspiration. Sometimes, I feel as though there is a part of me that's missing, like my artistic sense. Maybe once I get that back, I'll start drawing," I said to him.

"Why do you think there's something missing? You have me!"

"I don't know... it kind of went missing after Mrs. Moon put us in that seating chart. I feel like I'm different, because nobody can obsess over a seating chart as much as I did. It feels like something is wrong."

He kissed the picture, placed it on a huge piece of paper, set up my charcoal pencils, fluffed the pillows on my seat, and he said, "Well, make sure to complete this before we get married. I want to present it at our wedding."

Back in January, I stared at the empty paper. And now, I am still staring at this empty piece of paper, crying out to me. I had nothing better to do, so I grabbed my pencil, and started expressing myself. Drawing relaxed me, for the first time in awhile too. It made me forget about the presentation, for the first time in awhile too.

As the final days of school approached, the thought of summer vacation is on my mind. Going to the beach, shopping sprees, hanging out with friends, and studying early for the prep school I got into. I may never see Coraline or Clevis again, or be in a seating chart with them, but I will miss the memories we've had. I'll dream of the snow that fell, and The Wolves that howled, and I'll dream of my little friend stalking me. But for now, we have four days left, and there are only four days left, for these four days left, our presentation group has to focus for the four days left, for four days, that are left.

"Let's start the PowerPoint," I yelled to my so-called 'unlucky' square. They didn't listen because Mrs. Moon's room is a bouncy house, full of rowdy kids jumping on each other, and everybody screaming and talking, and not working. This bouncy house is bound to deflate soon, and I knew it in my heart that this room will soon explode.

"I know I know, my brain is also hyped up, but chop chop, we've got three days to complete this. If you know how to read a calendar, than you will know that today is Tuesday, three days until the presentation. Yesterday was good because we started planning the actual presentation. Oh yes, a very productive day yesterday, where we talked about what we'll wear, and what tones of voice we'll be talking in. Today though, we REALLY need to start working on this, because if you could hear my complete sarcasm, we did NOT have a productive day yesterday."

Once again, my group groaned like there is no tomorrow, even though the day after tomorrow and the tomorrow after that, we'll have nothing to present. It doesn't help that the pressure from Clevis being in here is making myself in a worse mood. Anything can happen between us, and with every action I do, I am always walking on eggshells that could hurt my feet and scar them for life.

I have one class with him, which is Science. Regularly, I have to be in the same room with him for an hour, and those periods were the worst after our dramatic break ups. Now that we have the same room assigned for our presentation groups, I have to spend about five hours here, with him, in the same room. It's like having Science five times, working on our solar system projects for triple the amount of time. This must be a nightmare for him, as it is for me. I am prepared for the worst of the worst.

It was after lunch when my brain healed, and I started to be in a better mood. We worked productively and our group agreed that I'd be the one to speak about it. Every so often, people from different rooms would come in and ask us debate questions for their topics. They'd get a feel for what our school would answer for that question. I enjoyed saying yes or no to them, and there were a lot of questions floating around. Charlotte came in and asked us if we swam with sea turtles, and Penelope asked us whether we should stay home if we have a cold or not, and a girl named Piper asked us about the textures of lettuce.

About a half hour before the last bell rang, the two musketeers proudly marched in, while the third one covered her face. When The Wolves walked through the door, their high heels clomped towards me. They are outshining the sun, but by now, they should be shining so much that they'll burn themselves. They better only be here to ask a question, and not a question about Clevis and I. I stopped answering those a long time ago.

"Minnie and your fellow group, we are asking everyone what their favorite store is. Then, we will research that store, and explain why the prices of the good quality products should be higher," Jill said. Higher? "Did you mean why they should have LOWER--?" Aneska growled. Victoria interrupted, like what she used to do with me.

"Seriously, this is the 21st century. We have money now, and it's not like we live in the Industrial Revolution. These high heels I'm wearing, they were only eight hundred dollars. If you look closely, than you'll see that this is real diamond. Diamonds for $800 is ridiculous, and those prices have got to get higher, so the quality of them can be better," she complained. She stomped on her precious diamond high heels.

"Minnie, what is your favorite clothing store?" Jill asked.

"Well, I really like that small place in town, I think it's called, something like, 'The Clothing Store', or something like that," I answered truthfully. That is where I buy most of my old-fashioned clothes. Everything there is set back a generation behind us. The generation of plaid shirts, high waisted jeans, and where people could buy comfy clothes without caring. That is my kind of style, but since we are in this generation, I am considered brave by saying that.

Everyone heard what I said and started giggling. The two populars started laughing so hard, and Victoria laughed so hard that she tripped onto the floor. Those high heels aren't trustworthy or precious. They just hold the feet of a (really bad swear word). Their laughing made everyone else laugh, and I'm simply used to this by now. I slapped my forehead in shame, because once again, I've said the wrong thing.

"I like 'The Clothing Store' too," Rogelio defended. Rogelio wears plaid almost every day, and on the other days, he'd wear a t-shirt from there. This is getting heated... from all the laughter going around. By now, people were falling out of chairs. In this generation, we have three common things. This generation likes to wear the same clothing. The second thing is this generation judges each others clothing. The third and final thing applies to me. Any outcast who doesn't wear that type of clothing will get made fun of.

"Ohh, you two lovebirds have so much in common! You should date each other!" Victoria screeched. Another thing about our generation, a boy and a girl can't be friends with each other. If they smile or wave to each other in the hallway, than they'll be considered, 'dating'. Rogelio looked uncomfortable after people started chanting our names. Truth is, I can imagine us being a couple, but we are friends, and only friends, and friends is all we'll ever be, despite the night of the middle school dance.

I cried with laughter. But here, am I laughing, or am I crying? The world may never know, just like how they don't know how many licks it takes to get to the center of a tootsie pop.

"Well, she would date anyone just because Minnie is SO DESPER- ATE!!! IN FACT, I THINK WE CAN ALL BELIEVE THAT SHE HAS A MENTAL DISABILITY!!" Clevis shouted, above all the chanting. The room is silent for only a few seconds. In those few minor seconds, his words struck me, right in the core of my heart.

Yes, an explosion happened, the bouncy house deflated, and I am reunited with this issue. Everyone exploded with laughter, but I exploded with every other mixed emotion then laughter. I covered my face, hoping for somebody to help me climb out the abyss. I let myself fall, and as my face is covered, I heard the shrieks and screams out of everybody. I peeked through my fingers to find The Wolves patting Clevis on the back. He is laughing his ankles off, so what am I now, a laughing stock? A thing that people could make fun of for liking a different store, or for being different, even though it's not my fault? My face is as red as a tomato, but that tomato is in a odd shape, perhaps a squash. Clevis just squashed me, and my vegetable garden died from heatstroke. I knew something like this would happen, but I never expected for this to happen.

Finally, is that what Clevis thinks of me after this? Desperate, autistic, having a mental issue, that I dated him because of it? Desperate is a strong word, almost as strong as the word, love. The definition of desperate is: tried in despair or when everything else has failed; having little hope of success. My own definition of desperate has autism written all over it.

Everybody else didn't think of desperate as an offensive word, and even though they thought my issue is a joke, nothing will change the fact that Clevis told everybody. Another thing to add onto the list of things I hate about this generation. People laugh at the fact that I have a disability, and they think nothing of it.

The only person who isn't laughing is Mrs. Moon. In the few seconds of silence before the room exploded, Mrs. Moon covered her mouth and rushed right towards the phone. Nobody else noticed her say Clevis' name. She looked very concerned, which also made me more concerned.

But what did I do? Covered my face, slumped into my chair, wanting this to stop, even though it wouldn't stop. It will never stop. That is the truth.

"   Min, Mrs. Moon wants you to go outside with her," Rogelio whispered. He pointed to the door and there is Mrs. Moon, looking straight at me. She nodded her head towards the hallway and indicated me to follow her. I got up from my desk and Mrs. Moon closed the door once we were outside. Clevis is nowhere in sight.

"Lets go to the room next door. I think we need to talk," She insisted. Mrs. Moon lead me into the empty and abandoned science room next door. The walls were plain and there is a single table in the center of the room. She sat down in one seat, and I sat in the other. Mrs. Moon hesitated for a moment, and my face heated up.

"   What is the last thing Clevis said before I took him out?" Mrs. Moon inquired, in a serious tone. Mrs. Moon never uses a serious tone. She only does when something really concerns her, or if we turn in our homework late. Either way, she knew this is a serious thing.

"He… he... he said that I, am desperate, with a mental disability," I choked.

"That's right, and that is also why I sent him to the dean," She stated. I stared at her in shock.

"Why there??" I yelled in a soft tone. He did deserve to get into trouble, but not to go to the detention room, where the dean will probably crack his knuckles with a ruler. That's where the really bad kids go.

Mrs. Moon took a deep breath. "I sent him right to that room because that comment concerned me. He may not know how bad it really is, but the word desperate means a lot, and not in a good way. I mean… it's a good thing nobody suspected what is really going on with you… and only I know that you are half autistic," She started.

"You KNEW?!"

"When you were younger, I worked at your preschool. Over the course of that year, I noticed you were different. You'd obsess over certain things, you would interpret stuff wrong, and, you were overthinking

A LOT. I told your parents about this, and then you were diagnosed. You got an IEP, and I switched to this school. However, when I got you this year, I was so excited! This year, I saw you for the person who you truly are. You are an artist, you are unique, quirky, smart, and you ARE a front row person. But yes, I knew that you were autistic, the whole time," She admitted. "I've noticed it this year when your mind seems to... overexaggerate these things. The Wolves aren't perfect, everybody's lives didn't depend on your relationship with Clevis, and the seating chart did not start this. It's like you live in a new world where you exaggerate everything, thinking it's real. Your mind is making a molehill into a mountain, meaning, you think differently than others. That can be beneficial, and not."

"Valentine's Day. I regretted that... and I can't really explain why I did it, but I guess I was only mad at myself... or... I'm not sure," I mumbled.

"It's okay, but you have to understand that I went home all messed up. I was upset, confused, and I was worried about you. You wouldn't or couldn't understand that. That's when I knew your autism had something to do with it. You see Minnie, it's not your fault you're this way."

"Mrs. Moon, but what if autism really defines me?? Just think back to all the events that happened this year. I got back together with the person I broke up with. I made so many mistakes and hurt so many people. What if I did it all just for the attention? The popularity? I was a star when I dated him, but then so many things happened this year, and I've always been desperate for a boyfriend and popularity, to feel normal for once. I made all these dramatic decisions and most of them backfired, and sometimes, I don't know that I've hurt people. It's like I live on my own planet, with my own interpretations, and ways of communicating with each other. I am just autistic and nothing else," I cried.

"Clevis isn't wrong."

"The autism spectrum is gigantic, and this affects you in the tiniest way! There are people out there where this is actually a problem, but you're normal enough to recognize these things. You are in between being fully autistic and being normal. I think you're just... confused. You're just..."

"In the middle," I finished.

Mrs. Moon put both her hands on my shoulders and brought me closer. "Minnie, autism doesn't define you because you are just, YOU. This is your personality, and it's special the way it is. You have this creative sense, and you can use this autism to help improve yourself. One good thing about being in the middle is that you're aware of the things going around you. You are different from everyone else, you feel differently, and you think differently, and that can be beneficial in the worst of times. And that snowy owl you've been imagining... the snowy owl is a higher frequency of owl symbolism. It's connected with magic and the mysteries of the universe - to see beyond the illusion of time and reality. It represents ascension of the soul to higher levels of thought and consciousness. It represents spiritual influence, wisdom and knowledge. It represents you as a person. Clevis shouldn't have said that though. He knew what would get you deep down," Mrs. Moon whispered. She gently walked her hands down my arms, as I am taking all of this in. It is a lot. All I could do is nod.

"I want to apologize," Mrs. Moon said sorrowfully. "I should have thought twice before putting you in that seating chart. I had a feeling something like this would happen, and I never expected for you two to start dating, and I also never expected this situation. I thought that by doing this, I can get you out of your comfort zone, and make you see the person you truly are. I know you don't love yourself, but I do want you to. I want you to see this as a gift, instead of a disability. In fact, it should be called an ability, because there are many great things you can do with this, but that is for you to figure out. It looks like you were right Minnie. A seating chart can affect you in so many ways, and I put you in the middle of it all."

"I should start calling myself… the girl in the middle. That suits me."

That same night, I sat at my desk, thinking, like how I am always overthinking now. After all the things Mrs. Moon said, my inner owl is migrating out of my cold self. Clevis is completely right, because who would want a desperate kid with a disability in this world. I took an eraser, and erased the outlines of myself out of the school portrait. Many tears went into my pillow that night, and the scene from today kept on playing like a continuous record player. And, it is all because of a seating chart.

The sun shined brighter and grass grew greener. Cherry blossoms blossomed, and the birds chirped once more. Daffodils grew in my yard, the ocean is warming up, the world around me is much more healthy. That's what happens in the Springtime, and in springtime, it is a fresh new start, at least for the plants and animals. From the transformation of Winter, to Spring, and to Summer, our life comes back to us. The weather gets warmer, days are longer, and life inside a classroom is better. Inside a classroom, we have this sense of pleasure that summer is almost here. We only have three days of school left.

I took a seat in my square group. I looked around for Clevis, who could be lurking anywhere in this room, secretly telling people about my disease. I have to be making sure that I sit as far away from him as possible, preferably because of what happened yesterday. I looked and looked around the room, but didn't see him, or his group of so-called friends. I curiously looked at Mrs. Moon, who is staring at me. She smirked.

"You didn't!"

"I did," She reassured. Clevis and his group got assigned to another room, and it is all because of what happened yesterday. After talking to Mrs. Moon, and taking a mental walk around the school, there was five minutes before the bell rang. I walked back into the classroom, and Clevis wasn't there. I didn't expect him to come back that day, but I also expected him here today.

"Do you know what Mrs. Moon? I am glad you sent Clevis to that room. It was not right for him to say that," I sighed. I hope he'll learn his lesson, because I now believe that what he said is wrong, even though it is right. It is like a tricky multiple choice quiz, because you never know what's right, or what's wrong. You turn in a blank sheet, like how I also blanked out after the comment.

"I was concerned, and you should be too. We ladies have to stick together in these situations! If something like that ever happens in my room, then it is right to send him out. I am your teacher and have to make sure you are comfortable and safe. Remember, you have to put yourself before others in these types of situations. I can see that you have trouble doing that," she quoted.

Mrs. Moon went back on her computer and I relaxed in this 'Clevis-free-zone'. After twenty three hours, I recovered from his comment, and thankfully, nobody in this room said anything to me. The Wolves ignored me at lunch as much as I ignored them.

"Let's make this the best presentation ever. We have to work together!"

And so we did. We worked, and we worked some more. We worked as hard as the president works, in fact, we worked as hard as all the presidents of the 195 countries combined. We made a script for Rogelio and I to read off of while presenting. I am still having a hard time coming up with a speech about having a relationship, and after yesterday, I just didn't know what to say for that.

As we are putting on our final details, our group decided to take a break. "Good job team. We did well," I said, as a qualified leader. We all clapped at each other. Knowing that we are whipped into shape, we moved out of our square and to Mrs. Moon's desk, to tell her we finished.

Right when I am about to speak, Clevis barges in the room, almost breaking the door. He raced into the room as though he's getting chased by a mastermind criminal, but Clevis, I think you barged into a room with a mastermind mind criminal. "EVERYONE, I NEED TO KNOW IF WE SHOULD DANCE ON STAGE, OR SING ON STAGE."

Jill walked in. "Clevis, we aren't doing any of those things, now please try to listen to our group," She said. Jill grabbed his hand and pulled him out of the room. I'm not sure if I heard her correctly, but I think she said 'our' group. That explains a lot, and now, he's doing fashion prices with the Victoria gang. Surprising, because he doesn't have a fashion himself.

"Wow, he is so animated," Mrs. Moon shared.

"You are so right," I agreed.

Aneska chimed in "My old science teacher hated him. In sixth grade, he was in my science class. One day, it was after lunch and Clevis had a bunch of sugar or something like that. He got on the table, and danced like a drunk Irish person would. My science teacher was out of the room and came back to find him ripping up his science papers. This was the day before Christmas vacation, so while ripping up papers, he sang Jingle Bells and claimed he was making snowflakes." Mrs. Moon is shocked, covering her mouth.

"He tried to threaten me with a knife," Coraline said. I engaged myself into her story and every word. The whole time, Mrs. Moon's face is speechless as she learned more about the Clevis events throughout the years. "This happened in elementary school. Yes, I've known Clevis for a long time, which is unfortunate because he made me into the person I am today. One day, he asked me to do something for him, like he wanted to borrow a pencil or something like that. Clevis just said, 'DO IT OR I HAVE A KNIFE IN MY BACKPACK' He said to the class. Remember, we were children, and he was very immature at that moment. Turns out, he didn't have a knife in his backpack after the principal searched for it," Coraline said.

"Did he actually do that??" Mrs. Moon asked. Coraline nodded and then, we kept on telling stories and laughing about it. I'm just here listening to Clevis' background story, and I am astounded. More people joined our conversation and soon, this is a whole class discussion.

"Well, there was this thing once, it was called couple counseling," I began. Only Aneska and Coraline knew what I am referring too, so they broke out laughing.

"That was the best, but at the same time, it was the worst experience," Coraline said. Ah, the old memories, coming back to life, as I tried to forget them. Coraline explained to the class what happened in couples therapy, and the whole time, it's like watching a teenager's emotional roller coaster. Their reactions are similar to mine, and for a moment, I felt like one of them, living through my own experience, yet, it's a whole other story.

"Do you have any other stories you would like to share about Clevis," Aneska asked. Everyone in the class looked at me, as I'm about to tell one story of Clevis. There are so many stories out there, each with new chapters. New plot twists, and dramatic moments, and several climaxes. I only said one word, that had a million meanings and definitions.

"Science."

Mrs. Moon almost fell out of her chair. "Why? Whatever happened in here?"

"And then there was that one time he complimented me for my drawing of Jupiter during class," I remembered. "He specifically stated that he wanted to be as good as me."

"Well, you are an amazing artist. I've seen your instagram posts and all of them are just so spectacular!" Aneska said. Most people agreed, but then they went back to work, knowing that the interesting part of our class discussion is over.

"Have you seen any of Minnie's artworks?" Coraline asked Mrs. Moon.

"I have just been waiting to see one of them," Mrs. Moon said, pleading to show her one of my artworks. Rogelio also urged to me to show him, so I whipped my phone out and showed my art album to them. On my phone, I have a separate album of all my genius artworks. The ones that would awe people. To make them say, 'amazing'. It feels great to receive compliments like those, and not only that, but I used to express myself through those paintings. It is like if somebody writes a memoir, they can express their feelings through words, and people can understand that. Through my art, I have the ability to express myself and my personality through images, it may just be a thing autistic kids can do, but I have a gift for that. I showed Mrs. Moon and Rogelio the picture of the snowy owl I drew. Mrs. Moon thought it is extraordinary.

"Are you working on anything right now?" Mrs. Moon asked. I mostly drew a lot B.T.S.C., before the seating chart. In that era, I drew all the time. I'd spend hours a night with the tiniest details, and create masterpieces. Now that it's A.T.S.C. (After the seating chart), I haven't had time or inspiration, but I'm slowly moving through the portrait now.

"Well, I am working on one thing right now. I am drawing a portrait of our school on a gigantic piece of paper," I babbled.

"Wow, that sounds awe-inspiring!" Mrs. Moon said. She hesitated for moment, then lit up like a light bulb. "I have an idea to share, with just you," She said, shooing the others away. She leaned in closer and whispered something into my ear.

"Yes."

"Almost."

She continued to whisper into my ear until my face glowed. The other kids still hanging around had a confused expression on their faces. "So, back to work everybody," Mrs. Moon said, changing the conversation. She smiled at me, and her eyes twinkled, kind of like the owl's. I breathed in and out, missing my tiny friend.

What Mrs. Moon said to me made me the happiest middle schooler in Center Middle School. How I can present my portrait at the presentations, then how she'll hang it up, where everybody could see it. Tonight, I finished the outlines of the drawing, adding more detail, texture, and taking all of today's compliments to heart, like I always do, and like I always will.

I hate public speaking, whether it's participating in class, or giving a presentation to the whole school. As much as I hate being in the spotlight, I also get a sense of satisfaction afterwards. That is a fact I learned from the events with Clevis this year, and the musical, and finally, presenting the solar systems project. For other people, it is more of a common fear most people have. Mostly, the shy people are afraid to talk to their friends, and the slightly less shy people are afraid to talk in front of their class. Today though, loads of people are going to hate today, because hence, presenting our solar system projects.

My head is spinning like the second hand on a clock, but much faster, like the mili-second part of the clock. My mind twisted and twirled knowing that I would speak. I am used to being in the center of attention by now, but this is for half of an exam grade.

As I walked into her room, I stormed to her desk.

"Mrs. Moon, WHY are you making us present our projects during a preparation for an exam?"

"Would you rather do it tomorrow, right before your bigger presentation?"

She does have a good point, so I shook my head, groaning. Unlike the other days where our presentation groups would come in and start working, our science class is reunited one last time. The desks are set up like a theater, in rows, but tilted so the audience can have a better view. While that part of the room is dark, the front is filled with light, made for the person whose in the spotlight.

Our group is up first, so the next thing I know, I'm standing next to Coraline, and next to Coraline stood Clevis, who continuously glared at me. They both looked at me, because as we agreed before, I'd be the person who'll be talking. Mrs. Moon had her grading sheet ready with a pencil in her fingers. The whole class is staring at me, and I stared at them. Our PowerPoint is projected on the screen, and it's like I'm in the center of the stage, forgetting my lines and absolutely panicking. Now I remembered to introduce us, the group in charge of the moon.

"Hello everybody, my group is doing the moon, and we are Minnie, Coraline and Clevis," I said, putting myself in the third person. Usually after I introduce myself, things are calmer, and smoother. I relaxed a little and leaned back on the wall, hoping this sort of a thing doesn't happen tomorrow.

"The moon is the easiest celestial object to find in the night sky -- when it's there. Earth's only natural satellite hovers above us bright and round until it seemingly disappears for a few nights. The rhythm of the moon's phases guided humanity for millennia -- for instance, calendar months are roughly equal to the time it takes to go from one full moon to the next. Moon phases and the moon's orbit are mysteries to many. For example, the moon always shows us the same face. That happens because it takes 27.3 days both to rotate on its axis and to orbit Earth. We see either the full moon, half moon or no moon (new moon) because the moon reflects sunlight. How much of it we see depends on the moon's position in relation to Earth and the sun. Though a satellite of Earth, the moon, with a diameter of about 2,159 miles (3,475 kilometers), is bigger than Pluto. (Four other moons in our solar system are bigger.) The moon is a bit more than one-fourth (27 percent) the size of Earth, a much smaller ratio (1:4) than any other planets and their moons. This means the moon has a great effect on the planet and very possibly is what makes life on Earth possible," I read off the slide, stealing some information from space.com. As I read more and more, I got calmer and calmer, like the waves at low tide, caused by the shining solid in the night sky.

I read off another slide Clevis wrote, and heard some giggling. I kept on reading and a few seconds later, there is more giggling. At that moment, Victoria melodramatically bursted out with laughter. After her, so did everybody else. I wasn't doing anything wrong, or funny. This is my education on the line, so I'm urgent about this.

"CLEVIS!!" Mrs. Moon shouted. I stopped reading and turned to him at the speed of light. He held his hand up and is pretending it's my mouth. He did the annoying 'Minnie is blabbering on and on' thing. An ugly impression on my presentation, and I know he hates me but he just crossed the line.

"RED CARD," he yelled, blushing. A soccer player who has been cautioned may continue playing in the game; however, a player who receives a second caution in a match is sent off (shown the yellow card again, and then a red card), meaning that he must leave the field imme-diately. Clevis gave me a red card, telling me to leave the field. I desire to kick a soccer ball in his face, that will be my next goal.

As I watched everybody laugh, I saw the people they really are. There's Victoria, who only seeks attention, and the other Wolves, fol-lowing in her lead from the fright of her eating them. There's Coraline, trying to cover Clevis' mouth, who I can call my friend. Mrs. Moon, like the moon watching over our actions, and creating a light in the sky when there's a dark problem. And Clevis, hiding something deep inside him, making him imitate me, the wise owl, who keeps on traveling to places in the world. Whether it is the world of grief, or the world of happiness, there is an owl, floating around someplace.

That night, my eyes fluttered to my pencils in my room. Those solid black charcoal pencils can make textures out of anything. With differ-ent shades and lines, who ever knew that pencils could change lives. I'm sure a simple and singular pencil changed an artist's life, because after I started drawing, my life changed. I got the inspiration I needed, especially after what happened today. But I didn't just draw a portrait, I drew how I see my school, from my point of view. I stared at the school picture we took in November. A month before A.T.S.C., our team was posing for the picture outside. My friends were both yelling to me from the middle. They waved for me to come over, but I refused because it was too late to move spots and the picture was taken. I felt insecure about moving to the middle, knowing I'd be in the center of attention if I moved at the last minute.

My pencil moved around carefully, sketching everything my mind crossed. With every object I drew, I sank a little lower into my seat and my muscles relaxed as I kept on drawing and drawing. I worked on it for about two hours and went to bed excited to see what tomorrow would bring to me.

May 5th is Cinco De Mayo. To Mexico, Cinco de Mayo is an annual celebration held on May 5. The date is observed to commemorate the Mexican Army's unlikely victory over the French Empire at the Battle of Puebla, on May 5, 1862, under the leadership of General Ignacio Zaragoza. And to us Americans, a day to eat Mexican food. The only day of the year when the Mexican restaurants have a wait, and the only day where I can wear a sombrero to school. To myself, Cinco De Mayo will be the saddest day of my life, because of two things. For one, I'm going to fail at this presentation, and two, the day I say goodbye.

Here is a famous quote I heard a lot in my childhood: all things that are good have to come to an end. This quote demonstrates that time doesn't stop for you, the world doesn't revolve around you. Even if you are having the best of times, time keeps on going on and on. Soon, whatever you're doing, or whatever good thing you're in, it will end at some point. The last of anything is an emotional time, whether it is the last few minutes of somebody's life, or when the last day of school rolls around.

Most students are excited for school to be over, and the teachers are ecstatic about summer. As for myself, today will be one of the big-

gest days in my history book. I get to present my drawing to the whole
school. I looked at the magical piece of paper, that would be hanging on
a bulletin board in a few hours.

I wore a black dress. I'm not going to a funeral, but it feels like I
am. I looked in the mirror and I found something different than myself.
I see a woman, whose been through a hell of a time. A woman wearing
a solid black dress, who is starting a new chapter of her life today. I see
a woman full of understanding, compassion, and uniqueness, only, I
didn't believe it myself.

As I walked into school for the last time, I gripped onto the completed drawing, ready to present. My group is scheduled to be the last
one. Mrs. Moon thought our idea is very dramatic, so she is saving 'the
best for last'. I hope that somebody like Mrs. Moon, will keep that portrait for years to come.

When I walked into Mrs. Moon's room for the last time, I'm about
to bawl my eyes out. I sat in my square group, in the desk closest to
the front row. I felt like talking to the desk, talking about our memories
together, however, it would look strange if I talked to it. It's not a he or
a she, it is an object, but an object that changed my life. I left this exact
same desk on December 2nd, and look at me now. Sitting in it on the
last day of school. Is this a coincidence? I don't think so.

For the morning presentations, Clevis' group went first. They explained why the store prices should be higher, and nobody else agreed
with them. It's nice to see Victoria embarrass herself, like how she
embarrassed me when I had to sing in science. What I found strange is
that Clevis continually looked at me throughout the presentation. He's
the speaker of the group, and while speaking, he twirled his left leg. He
is nervous, twirling, and blushing at me.

Finally, at lunch that same day, Clevis comes to my table. The
Wolves gather around us, and I give him a strange look. Coraline

snarled. Clevis cleared his throat and said, "Minnie, I miss dating you. Can we get back together?"... holy swear word.

Chapter 12

The dictionary defines 'middle', as in, at an equal distance from the extremities of something. Or when you are in the center of something. My own definition of it is when you used to be in the middle of a seating chart, and it affected your life in so many ways, until you are once again, in the middle.

The dictionary defines 'tension' as when you're in a mental or emotional strain, or when you're in the state of being stretched tight. My own definition of it is when you're standing around the perimeter of the room, waiting to find out where your new seat in Science class will be. It is hard to believe that just a few moments before, I had been practically skipping into Mrs. Moon's classroom, a huge smile across my face. I had expected today to be a normal Friday at Center Middle School, with myself basking in my front row seat. I loved being in the front row, even if I wasn't exactly enthusiastic about the bland astronomy unit we were studying. My front row seat is my throne, where I felt unique and dominant, like the teacher's chosen pet. Unlike myself, all of the popular kids seemed to head to the back of the room, to get as far away from their teacher as possible. But not me, the front row is where I have been since school started, and now, months later, where I hoped to stay.

"Happy Friday students. Today, I'm going to place you in a new

seating arrangement," Mrs. Moon announced. Students stood along
the outskirts of the room, clutching their binders, laptops, and books
as if they were protective armor. The lonely desks looked back at us. I
leaned against the wall, and dread split over me like spilled water on my
sketchbook. A new seating chart is any student's worst nightmare, to a
person like me.

As Mrs. Moon walked towards the back of the room, and the tension grew like a building wave ready to crush upon the innocent sand
below. She faced the back row, with her teacher's pointer finger out and
ready to fire.

Imagine yourself in the climax of a movie, with the antagonist rising. I'm the protagonist, in agonising pain, Mrs. Moon controlling it.
The smirk on her face made me want to crumple like a piece of paper. I
stared at the last three people left. Clevis, the distracting and somewhat
demented class clown, and to Coraline, the goth girl with FAILING
grades. I gulped, glancing at the last open seats. Well, I lived a good
fourteen years.

"Coraline, Clevis, and let's put Minnie in the middle!" Mrs. Moon
exclaimed. While the science class is on Earth, myself, Coraline, and
Clevis are on another planet. Now, and forever, I am in the back row,
with two monkeys sitting right and left of me. I'm a lone wolf.
I'm just the girl in the middle.

My story starts with a seating chart. A simple seating chart, where
nobody could predict my future with it. A simple seating arrangement
that caused me to be in this situation. Clevis asked me to get back
together with him, after a break up, and a break up before that. I am in
the center of attention, all eyes are on me, hesitant to make a quick decision. People are chanting our names, and the hope of our relationship is
still alive, even though I thought it was dead. I wore black today for the
funeral of this, but the spirit and soul still arises.

I did the only logic thing, and ran away. I grabbed my yearbook, my phone, and my dignity, and ran away from my life. I couldn't say yes or no. Either way, people would've been hurt. Jill is watching, and pleading for Clevis not too, but he did, he asked me to make a life decision. I ran to my comfort place, and I never thought I'd be running through Mrs. Moon's door ever again. She's packing up her stuff, and the room is a mess. Her room and I are very similar, from the darkness it held, to the unorganized posters off of the walls. I stood right below Pluto, where I felt colder than all the planets combined.

"Minnie!? What's wrong!?" she asked, concerned. I dropped my stuff in the back row, and took a seat. I sat in the exact desk where I sat in that seating chart. Mrs. Moon sat in Clevis' old desk, and I explained to her the whole story. "Now, apparently, he wants to get back together with me..." I faltered. A teardrop splashed on the desk. Mrs. Moon is shocked, but hesitant for a moment.

"Give me your yearbook," She asked, holding out her hand. I realized I'm holding my yearbook, and gave it to her. She whipped out a black sharpie, and gripped my yearbook. I heard the sharpie scrap against the yearbook I got this morning. In the yearbook, is the memories I'll have forever. All the pictures of everyone in the school. I will never forget this year, ever. She handed the book back to me, and I'm expecting a typical teacher signature.

"Minnie, astronomy is the best, peculiarly when I purposely put you in the back row. Being in the middle means you know what is going on ahead and behind you. You have true potential, and you'll always be in the middle of something. In the middle of a seating chart, or in the middle of your own world. Own that world, live your life to its fullest, and next year, I'm banning the seating chart. I have a good reason for it too. -Mrs. Moon."

I smiled at her, and she squeezed my shoulder.

"Think about the past, present, and future when making an important decision. Where do you see yourself with Clevis in a month? Finally, being in the middle also means being aware of your surroundings. You're a middle girl, you can see left and right, forward and back, negative and positive, autistic and non-autistic. I consider that a gift you have. The only thing you should be concerned about is the happiness for yourself, and putting yourself first. And that's right, I did think twice before putting you in the seating chart, because I'm hoping that by the end of the year, you would realize that you are special for the person you are. It may have been a little experimental on my part, but isn't what science is for? To discover things?" Mrs. Moon inspired. Perhaps I'm not as bad as I thought I was...

After thanking Mrs. Moon, I was almost out the door when I turned to look at the window; I felt something staring. And indeed, I was right. The orange feather gleamed in the sunlight, the snowy owl brightened. Her golden eyes stared into mine and I got her message.

"You're just the girl in the middle," I heard her whisper.

"Yes, yes I am my little friend."

She flew away, one last time, to the moon hanging over the horizon.

"Hello Center Middle School!" I exclaimed. Here I am, on the stage, in the center of attention, in the middle of the room, and at the climax of a situation. The school quieted down, and I spotted close to one hundred people. While they quieted down, Rogelio, Aneska, and Coraline are over to the side, giving me a thumbs up. I gripped the printed papers I held, then I ripped them, making Mrs. Moon chuckle. Than I turned our PowerPoint off, making my group shocked. Rogelio held out his packet in question, and I refused to take it.

"What I'm going to say to you will be straight out of my heart. I don't need a paper to read off of, I just need to speak," I spoke into the microphone. I took the microphone off of its stand, and placed myself in center stage.

"First off, let me introduce my topic. We are doing the significance of relationships. If you're wondering, then yes, this is my idea. My group agreed with me, because this is a good subject to talk about and explain since we're all going into high school next year. As most of you know, Clevis and I, we were together once. As a couple, a middle school couple. There aren't many middle school couples, which made us popular. But after that, I strive for attention. Before we got together, I have always wanted popularity, and a boyfriend. In fact, I am so desperate for it. I got an opportunity when Mrs. Moon put me in the middle of a seating chart. That science seating chart is where I fell in love with Clevis," I introduced. I looked at him, who is fully engaged. Clevis had a gleam and a grin on his face. His hazel eyes twinkled in the light.

"Now, what I have to present to you is a portrait of this school. If you have eyes, then you can see that there are no humans in this picture. No people, no faces, or a school. That's right, this is how I see us, from the perspective of an autistic girl. Instead of drawing people, I drew the moon, a tree, a rock, and wolves howling. Because my brain is wired in a different way, I expressed my thoughts through drawing. Now give me a chance to explain what I see."

"Coraline, ever since Mrs. Moon placed you next to me in the seating chart, you remind me of a tree, growing everyday, turning over new leaves, and I am proud to call you my best friend," I said to her.

"I'll teach you how to ride a motorcycle one day!" She shouted.

"Next, for The Wolves, always seeking the attention. You are on top of the rock, howling at the full moon, but then the moon disappears, and you go hiding into darkness. Wolves, if you're going to be like that, then I don't consider you leaders. You can stop making people upset to cover up the wrong things going on in your life," I said. They snarled at me, but only Victoria had an understanding expression. She quieted down the Wolves.

"Clevis, I don't have a single regret dating you. However, through all the memories and struggles we've had together, I can't imagine a future with each other. I didn't put you in the portrait because I can't see you in my picture of life. I have to make this decision on my own, and the answer is no. I love you for different reasons. You are the person who inspired me to draw this, to make new discoveries, and without you, I would be too scared to be presenting this at this moment."

Clevis is crying. Breaking a heart isn't easy, even if you have already done it twice already.

"Mrs. Moon, you are the moon. The wise object in this sky, lighting up everybody's problems. You taught me that we have to live our lives to its fullest, and to put ourselves first in difficult situations. I have always been a middle girl, and you helped me realize it by putting me in that seating chart. Being in the middle isn't easy, but there is the light at the end of the tunnel. When you fall into an abyss, it is nearly impossible for the whole place to be dark. I have the wings to let myself fly in and out, and I consider that a gift. My name is Minnie Ann Stickley-Adotte, and my gift is a developmental disability, by the name of autism. I think and react to things in an unconventional way, and I thought that was a bad thing, until now."

I'm hesitant for a moment. "Who in this room has some sort of a problem with themselves? Who doesn't like themselves for who they are, and who has a disadvantage they think people in this generation cannot accept?"

I raised my hand. At first, only a few people raised their hands, then a few more, and a couple more. After a few more seconds, almost half of the people in the room shot their hand up, soon to be almost all. The Wolves stayed silent, their hands in their laps and rolling their eyes.

"See? Almost everyone in this room has some sort of a problem, whether it's a serious disability, or just not accepting themselves," I practically yelled.

Coraline walked to me, and asked for the microphone. I gave it to her, almost in shock considering she would "rather die than speak in front of 100 judgemental people including The Wolves."

"Alrighty listen up folks! My name is Coraline. I don't have a last name because when I was very young, my parents abandoned me. Ever since then, I didn't have a last name so I went as Coraline Blank, and I felt blank until now. I suffered through depression through most of this year because I couldn't find good relationships with people, until my first friend, Minnie, came. See, the thing about relationships is to have significance in a relationship... is to have a good relationship with yourself first. You must love yourself, despite the disadvantages and disabilities you have."

I stated, "And, you can't use somebody else to help you with your problems, because that is for YOU to figure out. I am so sorry about that Clevis. I saw past your... immature behavior. And I caught sight of who you truly are. Would you like to come up here and tell everyone your point of view?"

Clevis looked shocked as he stood up. Well, that is a first.

"As most of you know, I have problems, whether it's shouting out in class, or creating drama like Minnie, or just wanting attention. I have a high case of ADHD, and I am on the spectrum a little, like Minnie. But you're right Min, it makes me unique, and not any worse than... The Wolves. I could maybe become a public speaker one day! Or a teacher! Someone who uses a loud voice everyday with tons of enthusiasm! This is who I am and I was and who I will be," Clevis said.

"One more thing. People who think they don't have any problems are The Wolves, and you guys think you can really judge and make fun of me for it? SERIOUSLY??" Clevis began. He started ranting and ranting about everything that happened this year and making good points about it. I am so proud of him.

I took the microphone once he started swearing.

"My point is, people who learn to accept their disadvantages are fearless, notable, remarkable, and personally, I consider any disability to be gift, because it makes us stand out. For us, we can see the light at the end of the tunnel, and the whole world in ways normal people could never understand. We learn to live a better life because problems make us acquire knowledge about ourselves. We may be different, but not any less amazing."

It is only then I realized the owl inside of me returned, and it returned to stay for a lifetime.

"Minnie, where are you in the portrait?" Clevis asked. After thinking he'd never speak to me again after making him talk in front of the school, he spoke a question I am wondering myself.

"You deserve to be in it," Coraline added on, walking towards us.

"You really think so?" I said.

"It's the only thing we both agree on," Clevis said, laughing. They gave me a pencil, and I drew the snowy owl, adding the orange feather on the tip of the tail. Not many owls have that feather, but it is something I am now proud of.

Coraline glared at the portrait again. "A snowy owl... are you making more cheesy metaphors in your head Min? Imagining stuff we can't? Drawing things that have to be explained? Is that just an autistic thing or..."

"You know Coraline, I think it's just me, myself, and I, and nothing else."

"But you're autistic..."

"And..." I raised an eyebrow. As I placed this picture on the wall, I placed myself in the middle of my life, like how Mrs. Moon placed me in the middle of an unlikely yet useful yet unique seating chart.

"Minnie Ann Stickley-Adotte..." Mrs. Moon started, storming over, ready to rave on and on about my presentation. She glanced at the snowy owl on the portrait, and paused. "....I like your minor adjustment. It makes the portrait more extraordinary."

"It really does," Clevis added on. "That owl is always in the center. I wonder if it's just a coincidence," he observed. I gleamed and beamed at them.

"Well, what do I know about being in the center?"

I'm just the girl in the middle.

About the Author

Cassidy Ferry is a self-proclaimed overachiever who started writing this book at the age of 13. With the help from numerous people, and the countless support she got, it took two years of school vacations, weekends and any free time she had to complete her first novel. Cassidy hopes this story will influence middle schoolers to be accepting of other people despite their differences. She lives in Wakefield, RI with her family and Saint Bernard dog named Minnie.

Acknowledgements

First, many thanks to the people in my old middle school who inspired this story. A special thanks to Mrs. Light for putting me in this seating chart to inspire a new twist of crazy events. And to the girl on the right and the guy on the end for helping me create this story. To all of the people who were like The Wolves, thank you for giving me the motivation to publish this book.

Thank you to my friends for always supporting me. Much appreciation towards my family especially my parents who made this possible.

An additional thank you to Mrs. Pezzelli, Mr. Martinez, Dr. Ferry (my Dad) and my friends who helped edit and revise my manuscript through these past two years.

Thank you to all middle schoolers, you will all be in the middle of something at some point in your life but perhaps that isn't such a bad thing.

This book is dedicated to Mrs. Ferguson for teaching me that writing is nothing more than a guided dream.

CPSIA information can be obtained
at www.ICGtesting.com
Printed in the USA
BVHW072111100119
537567BV00019B/170/P